DEADLY PRAYERS

By Pascal Littman

chicago
spectrum
press

Copyright © 1996 by Pascal Littman.

CHICAGO SPECTRUM PRESS
1572 Sherman Avenue • Annex C
Evanston, Illinois 60201
800-594-5190

ISBN 1-886094-45-4

Printed in the U.S.A.

10 9 8 7 6 5 4 3 2 1

To our husbands, Jerry and Armand, who took up cooking and seashells while we were occupied with murder and mayhem.

We want to thank Sgt. John Schmidt, now retired, and Detective James Spencer, Area 3, Violent Crimes Unit, Chicago Police Department, for their patience, time, and willingness to help in the research of this book.

"To die is poignantly bitter, but
the idea of having to die
without having lived
is unbearable."
— ERICH FROMM, *MAN FOR HIMSELF*

❧ ONE

The figure bent over the basket of spilling papers and garbage, rummaging almost delicately in the filth.

Because of the half-light between sunset and evening, the figure was not clearly male or female. Clothes didn't give it away either: tattered skirts over pants, a rumpled army jacket and a Bears cap. When the figure stood, however, the sodium street lights cast a pink glow over what was clearly a woman's face, but the bag-lady attracted little attention. The homeless of Chicago's Uptown neighborhood were constantly scrounging through rubbish for the big find: an odd boot, a torn glove, or a purse that had been grabbed, emptied and tossed. Some had everything they owned in their bags, others had only the day's take. Sometimes they found more than they were looking for.

The woman shuffled along the sidewalk, clutching her coat as she kept close to the lighted store windows. She ducked into a doorway when a gang of loud kids approached, their boombox throbbing a raucous salsa, and they danced by, as though the sidewalk was their private disco. When they left, she walked to the garbage can at the corner.

Someone was there ahead of her, an elderly black man, singing softly as he folded the newspapers neatly into a pile.

He pulled out a half-eaten candy bar, saw her out of the corner of his eye, and said, "This trash ain't too bad. Wanna try?" She shrugged. "Sure."

When he moved away, smacking his lips over the stale candy, she shoved aside the newspapers and empty soda cans and dug deeper into the waste. Feeling something hard in a plastic bag, she pulled it free.

It was an ordinary plastic bag, the kind used in supermarkets. She opened it to look inside just as two skate-boarders came racing down the sidewalk toward her. She jumped back and they laughed. "Move it, stinky lady," one hollered.

Bruised at the insult, she dropped the package, unopened, into a shopping bag and took off in the opposite direction.

The day was not going well. This was a rough neighborhood, and the bag lady needed to sit for a quiet moment. The sheltered bus stop was at the end of the block. The bench was unoccupied and no one was around. She sighed with relief. But a light rain began to fall, and between that and the dark, she was disoriented. She tried to read the street sign but the light was out, shot to death, no doubt.

Remembering the package now, she took it from the bag and tried to peel away the layers of newspapers. Her gloves were clumsy, and the papers were stuck fast by thick brownish clots, half-dried and slimy. She tore at the paper, determined to see what was inside. When the final fold was laid back, she gasped.

The object was white as chalk. A fetid stench coming from the clumps of dried matter went straight to her stomach, and she fought down the urge to be sick.

Even in the poor light she recognized the grisly object as a human hand. After a moment the queasiness passed, and she took another, closer look. It was a woman's hand, the white skin smooth and youthful. Manicured nails were long and painted a bright red, accentuating the slim, tapered fingers. A ring coiled around the third finger, a golden snake, green stone eyes catching the light with an unseemly dazzle.

She shivered, looking at the shreds of skin and tissue dangling from the severed end, arteries and ligaments and bones resembling so much plastic tubing.

She had seen enough, and quickly wrapped the wretched find back in the soiled paper and stuffed it into the bag. But it could not stay there.

What, she wondered, does one do with something like this. Call the police? She couldn't throw it back in the can, either. You just don't do that with somebody's hand.

Standing and collecting her possessions, she started walking. The rain was coming down harder now, chilling her even through the heavy clothing.

The shrill wail of a siren in the distance reminded her that St. Phillipi Hospital was only a few blocks away, and with sheets of rain flooding the sidewalks and streets, she broke into a run, the shopping bag slapping awkwardly against her leg.

She had to get rid of the thing in the bag. The heavy army jacket was soaked and beginning to weigh her down. This, along with the gym shoes and two layers of wool skirts, prevented her from running fast, and she cursed the weather and her bad luck.

She saw the hospital's emergency entrance at the corner of Wilson and Clarendon, and stopped to lean against the street sign. Now what? Run in and hand it to someone and say, "Here. I found this?" In some macabre way, it was almost funny. She was standing out in the rain smelling like a wet horse with someone's hand in her shopping bag.

A squad car pulled up to the emergency entrance and she shrank back into the shadows. Two policemen jumped out of the car and ran into the hospital.

Impulsively, she bolted to the squad car, flung open the door, and threw the entire shopping bag with its ghastly contents onto the front seat.

❧ TWO

Wednesday night, George Burning Tree waited on one of the slatted wall benches at Area Three Headquarters. He was told Detective Beltz would see him in a few minutes.

The "Chief" had been in the station before, so his presence caused little stir among the cops working at desks or passing through the room. Out on the street, however, he was an odd sight.

George was very tall, carrying his six-foot-six height gracefully on a heavily muscled frame. His smooth skin gleamed like burnished mahogany. Deep-set black eyes missed nothing, yet, to most people, were flat and unreadable. His straight hair was long, falling like black silk over broad shoulders. A mover by trade, he dressed neatly on the job, and tonight his shirt and jeans looked freshly ironed. Beltz had learned over time that George's brooding scowl reflected thoughtfulness rather than anger.

"C'mon in, Chief," Lieutenant Stanley Beltz called from the open doorway of his office.

George entered, watching Beltz walk heavily to his desk, and figured fewer trips to the deli for the older man were in order, but he wasn't the one to tell him. Beltz had put on weight over the summer, his belt now worn on the last notch.

The stocky detective was looking his age. But George chalked it up to serving and protecting for thirty years, then losing his wife last year.

Beltz sat on the desk top and waved the Chief to a chair. "How're things going, Chief?"

"Good."

"Still working?"

"Yep."

"No bad news?"

"Nope."

"Thanks for coming in." Beltz knew George Burning Tree well, knew he spoke little and that the pleasantries were over. "Thought you might help on something."

George nodded, his heavy lidded black eyes curious, no expression on his bronze, square-jawed face.

"Anything on the street about a missing woman?" Beltz asked.

"Who?"

"Her name is Verna Lake. Small, blonde, about twenty-four. Been living in Uptown since spring. Nobody knows where she's from. Landlady hasn't seen her since Saturday. She always paid the rent like clock work, and Monday it was due and she didn't show."

"Where?" Not a flicker in George's eyes.

Beltz checked in a notebook on the desk. "418 Kenmore. Apartment 3. You know the building?"

"Yes."

"You know the girl?"

"No."

Beltz looked up, his eyes narrowed. "You sure? I thought you knew everyone around here."

"Not her."

"She's clean, no sheet on her. Never caused any trouble. Quiet type. No one seems to know where she worked or if she even had a job "

George said nothing.

11

"Ask around, Chief. See what you can find out."

Beltz stood and put the notebook in his jacket pocket. "Ever get those basketballs the police wives sent over?"

George unwound his tall frame from the chair and stood. "Yeah, the kids used 'em last week against Lane Park. We won."

George had made points with Beltz a long time ago for his thoughtfulness, caring enough about the neighborhood boys to volunteer as their basketball coach. "You do good work at the Center, Chief. I hope they appreciate it."

"Maybe. Maybe not. But I like it."

Beltz walked with George to the stairs leading down to the first floor, and said goodbye. "Call me."

George left the lighted station quickly and rounded the corner onto a darkened side street. He passed a big hand over his sweaty brow.

Being an active snitch for Beltz had its drawbacks. Like tonight. Keeping a straight face when the cop says Verna's name right out loud. Missing? What the hell is that all about?

He lit a cigarette, inhaled deeply, and leaned against the side of the building. He knew Beltz was smart, smarter than the average detective at Area Three. Even after making Lieutenant two years ago, he continued to work homicides, sometimes with another man, mostly by himself. He was smart and he was fair, for a cop.

The detective had caught George along with two other boys trying to rob a small grocery store ten years ago. A kid then, the young Indian had insisted he only happened to walk in at the time of the robbery. The boys hated their new Indian neighbors and everyone knew it. They tried to implicate him, but George kept to his story. And Beltz believed him.

George owed the detective, and because he lived in Uptown along with many of his people, he agreed to help Beltz. And you don't foul your own nest. But he had to be discreet, come and go when few people were in the station.

Flipping the cigarette away, he noticed how his hands shook. He wanted to sit, but only slumped further against the hard brick wall.

What did he mean, Verna missing? She sure as hell was right where she belonged last Thursday night. Damn, that was one hell of a night. Unnoticed there on the dark street, he let his thoughts drift languidly to the sensual pleasures they shared then and every Thursday night for the last month. If there was a heaven, that was it. Crawling into bed with Verna was like entering the golden portals of paradise. Her flawless body, her skin so soft he could almost feel it now, and the bottomless bag of tricks to make him feel good.

Verna was one in a million, all right, an Uptown girl with the face like one of those angel statues in the church where the missionaries always dragged him as a kid. Christ, what a girl. He wondered again what she saw in him, so big and ugly and poor and usually scaring the girls away. But not Verna.

She was so eager to please, so receptive no matter what he wanted. Shit! How she loved it when he slammed inside of her, then she'd slow him down, begging him to tease her, in just a little bit, then out even slower, then back in again, now faster, harder, a blur of color with their brown and white skin kneading and pulling and writhing like one ecstatic animal, and then she'd let out that high scream when she came.

George's erotic daydream came to an abrupt and troubled end when he thought about his stupid lie. Shit! Why did he tell the cop he didn't know her? And where the hell was she?

He shoved his hands in the pockets of his denim jacket, hunched his shoulders forward, and began walking faster. Beltz would find out sooner or later that he knew her, but what else could he do. Verna asked him, hell, told him not to tell anybody about their fooling around. Intimacy, she called it. Don't tell anybody about our intimacy, Georgie, or it's all over.

He scowled, his black eyebrows knit together in one seamless line across his face. He had always helped the law, gone out of his way to give them information. As long as it didn't hurt any of his people. But this time it was different. This time, his own ass was on the line.

Shortly after George left, Molly Fast rushed into Area Three Headquarters. "I have an appointment with Lieutenant Beltz," she said to the desk sergeant.

"He sure is popular tonight," the sergeant muttered. "Come in, lady, take a seat." He motioned to a bench nearby. "He'll be with you shortly."

Molly sat down and glanced around, curious. This was her first time in a police station. The room was separated into a reception area and a larger space with desks and typewriters and telephones. Individual offices dotted the perimeter of the large room, most of them now occupied by night shift detectives. Some were busy talking or typing, others standing around a coffee machine munching on doughnuts and drinking from styrofoam cups. Two detectives were talking to a man holding a crying baby. The man kept putting a pacifier in the baby's mouth, and the baby kept spitting it out. Several uniformed officers moved in and out of the room and she could read the names on their jackets but knew she could never pronounce them; they all seemed to end in xjyz and ough.

"Well now," Stanley Beltz said, approaching her, "you must be Mrs. Fast."

"I was hoping...Lieutenant Beltz? ...that you...uh could help me..." Molly stumbled and hesitated, unsure and intimidated by the confusion in the station. She took a deep breath, appraised Beltz as a friendly man, his eyes keen, his manner confident. In his rumpled suit, frayed shirt cuffs, and full head of graying hair, he impressed her as believable and sympathetic.

"I'm a writer," Molly lied, "working on a book. I thought this neighborhood would be a good place to research."

"I see."

"This is your...bailiwick? District?" she stammered, "you must know everything that's going on here, let's say, after dark?"

"We try," he said, puzzled. " So, how can I help?"

"I need background, you know, everything I read in the paper...crimes, murders...and what they euphemistically call home invasions..."

"You really want to know all that sordid stuff?" He tried not to smile, and to be more patient.

"Sure. It sells books. Violence and glitz..."

"There's not much glitz around here, as you can see," Beltz rumbled, nodding to the chaotic scene outside his office. But she was a citizen and entitled to courtesy. "Come into my office...I don't know what you want. But I'm sure you'll tell me."

Beltz settled himself comfortably into his worn leather chair. "Take a seat. Exactly what did you have in mind ...that is, what I'm permitted to tell you."

Molly replied quickly, "How about a typical night? That sounds good. How about last night."

His eyes flickered. "Hm-mm, I'm afraid not, Mrs. Fast. There are legalities to consider...I can't be specific about cases. I can only give you a smattering of what our officers contend with. You'll have to accept that."

Molly could see this was going nowhere. He was within his rights and she knew it. Before he lost patience completely and dismissed her, she turned on the charm.

"Lieutenant Beltz," she said, smiling sweetly, "this book is very important and I want it to be as authentic as possible. Those generalities you spoke of...would you mind going into it a little bit for me? And my memory is so bad...could I tape it?"

Molly dug into her oversize purse and rummaged around, finally losing patience and turning it upside down on the desk. From its stuffed innards dropped a package of tissues, a lens cap, three rolls of unexposed film, a small tin of aspirin, an apple, a box of animal crackers, a huge ring of keys, a book of poetry and a tiny recorder.

She flipped the button on. "There. Just talk. What kind of a day was yesterday?"

Beltz leaned forward, his gray eyes lively with humor, and raised his voice for the mike. "Okay. I had eggs and bacon for breakfast, two slices of whole wheat…"

"Oh, come on," Molly said, laughing.

Beltz sighed, and reached to a shelf above his desk that was neatly stacked with law books and police journals. He began riffling through the pages of a small black book, trying his best to take her seriously. He figured her for late forties, but very different from most of the women he knew. So many of them had given up, let themselves go. This one had a certain flair. The long skirt and tunic sweater, a red silk rose pinned to its collar, hinted at a certain style.

But it wasn't just her clothes. It was the way she'd put herself together, her only make-up the slight outline of kohl around her eyes.

Aloud, he started reading: "The officer, out on the street with his partner, broke up a domestic quarrel. Husband drunk and yelling obscenities and with small kids in the house the neighbors were afraid and called us. When the officers arrived it was all over. The couple were lovey-dovey with each other." Beltz looked up. "You know, this happens a lot…our guys go in to break up a domestic disturbance and the people get upset and start yelling at the cops." He looked at his watch. "How'm I doing?"

She nodded.

"So they drove around a while," Beltz went on, "had dinner, Dispatch called about an alarm going off in an all-night grocery. The officers were lucky. The perp was just running out of the store…"

"Wait a minute. What's a perp?"

"Oh, sorry. Perp is a perpetrator. The person committing

the crime." He said it slowly, like a teacher explaining algebra to a small child.

She was annoyed. "Please go on."

"They booked him and went back out. Started searching for a little five-year-old kid who was missing. Jesus, I hate it when kids are missing. It was pouring last night, too.

"They found him just sauntering along like it was a bright sunny morning. There's this kid. Not crying, not afraid...just bopping along the sidewalk. So they pick him up and bring him to the station where his mommy comes and gets him, kissing and screaming at him at the same time. People!" He shook his head.

He stretched then, raising his arms and linking his fingers above his head. "So-oo...that's last night for you. Pretty typical. Got enough for your book?"

Molly stared at him. "That's all? Come on," she said finally, "there must be more."

He referred back to the log impatiently. "They had a call..."

"Where?" she urged.

"Why do you have to know that?"

"And...?"

His eye caught the little sign pasted on the tape recorder. He pointed to it. " 'Molly Fast,' " he read. " 'If you find me, call 236-FAST.' Does this thing get lost often?"

"Not if I'm attached to it," she said. "Can we finish?

"We're finished." He stood and closed the log.

"You holding anything back?"

"It was nice meeting you, Mrs. Fast. I hope I've been of some help."

"Lieutenant," she blurted, all the charm gone, "I'm not doing a book on hobo hamburgers or cooking with cheap wine. I wanted to talk to you because..." Molly stopped suddenly, realizing she was going too far. She didn't dare tell him the truth.

He waited.

She stuffed everything back into her purse and snapped it

17

shut. "I appreciate your help."

Molly flashed a bright smile that disarmed Stanley Beltz. He'd heard the irritation in her voice, but that he could handle. The smile was something else. Besides, anyone who reads poetry can't be all bad.

On her way downstairs, Molly fretted about the interview and how badly it had gone. He had been patronizing, treating her like a child, or worse, a crank. And she had taken it. Because there was so much more she wanted to know about the case. What clues did they have? Were they on to someone? How was she to ask all that without giving herself away.

After all, she was the one who had found the hand.

✺ THREE

Molly Fast was a new widow. Schuyler Fast had died eight
months ago, the greedy melanoma on his neck shattering a
thirty-year marriage in two weeks. He was the East Coast
lawyer who married the free-spirited artist and got his house
in the suburbs but with a fair trade-off; he had the prestigious
address, and she had the fun and a sense of style to make it
their home.

The hodge-podge furnishings ran from lion claws to
chrome and glass to mid-forties kitsch. Books spilled over
shelves, vases of fresh flowers and plants bloomed in every
room, and light poured through mullioned French windows.

They had laughed with every new acquisition, and when
he furnished the attic as a studio for her cameras and equipment, she gifted him with a robot. Dubbed Popeye, after one
eye fell out, the three foot animated butler carried a tray of
iced martinis and rolled through the living room like a tiny
alien. Sky had joked that if that's the kind of life on other
planets, we have nothing to fear.

When the laughter died with Schuyler, Popeye mourned
alone in a closet and Molly went back to work, taking her far-
out and original shots for the glossy magazines. She always
needed props, old, new, something unexpected to pop up in

the precise and carefully arranged sets.

Molly was a human filing system, her memory a catalogue of every thrift shop, flea market, specialty store and collector of absurd and whimsical trivia. She knew a man who owned garden statuary, from terra cotta squirrels to plastic monks to cement babies peeing in a fountain. She knew where to buy Christmas decorations in July, and how to wheedle toys and transparent yo-yos from warehouse security men. Life was a scavenger hunt, and the more ludicrous the thing hunted, the better she liked it.

She was after shock value in her photographs, something that didn't belong in the picture. But the older she grew, the harder it was to modify or displace that sense of the absurd. Her success defended it, or as Sky would have quoted Popeye, "I yam what I yam!"

It happened rarely that she wanted something she couldn't find. When it did, it sent her into questionable, sometimes unfamiliar neighborhoods. Last night's impersonation had been research for a job; she needed a bag-lady's cart and its contents.

She lay on her bed, still dressed as she had been for her appointment with the lieutenant. She glanced at the bedside clock. Midnight. Over twenty-four hours since she found that hand, its shredded tissue and decaying skin hanging from the crudely chopped wrist.

She closed her eyes and saw herself walking the streets of Uptown, the small grocery and dry-goods stores, taverns, pawn brokers, and vacant lots lining block after block. Empty buildings with black, cave-like windows, and rooming houses where bickering races and cultures lived in spray-painted squalor and constant violence.

These pitiless streets leading into the fancy hi-rises along Lake Michigan erected as if to hide all that decay. And she wanders into it like a fool.

She began to question last night's rash action. Should she have tossed the hand into the patrol car like that without explanation? The logical thing would have been to take it to the police, tell them where she found it, and not panicked. She sighed. There was no point in rehashing it.

But she couldn't forget the hideous dreams afterwards, throbbing with ugly, bloated, pulsating day-glo body parts inside a bloody whirlpool. When she tried to run, they melded suddenly, forming a grinning skeleton that reached out with bony fingers to grab her.

And then Fuzzy had telephoned the next morning as she worked in her studio, trying to capture the light on a stuffed red parrot. The ringing of the phone had startled her. "Too early for you Molly?" Fuzzy asked.

"No. I'm up."

"Will I have the proofs by the end of the week?" He paused. "I'm almost afraid to ask what that devilish brain of yours has cooked up this time."

"So don't ask."

"I'm asking."

"You'll see it. You know you like surprises, Fuzzy."

"Sure, sure, you always say that. I'll see the shots, I'll know."

Molly hung up. Fuzzy Hecht liked everything she did, the kookier the better. He was the rare easy client, a relief from some of the picky and demanding interior designers whose rooms everyone tried to copy. He liked it when she was outrageous. It was her trademark, and it made him look good.

Like finding that androgenous mannequin and arranging the naked limbs nonchalantly over the arm of a Baker couch, drink in one hand, cigarette in the other. Or the delicate and antique French provincial parlor into which she had centered a huge pink bean-bag chair with a sign in the seat: BE KIND TO YOUR TOOSHIE!

She sighed. Better finalize that layout soon or even patient Fuzzy might take his tooshie and his business elsewhere.

After his call, she remembered thumbing quickly through the Tribune, but there had been no word of a murder in

Uptown. And nothing on radio or television.

Maybe there was no murder. Maybe it was a horrendous argument with a ghastly outcome. Or maybe an accident. Or maybe just another statistic in the big city, something she'd never get used to.

Schuyler would have laughed at her costume last night, the dime-store wig and his shoes fitting her like clown's feet. He would have thrown his head back and roared. "My God, Molly, you're sexy as hell! If you don't leave this minute, I might ravish you right here on the floor!"

Molly chuckled. It was comforting to know that whatever she did, no matter how risky or flamboyant, Sky would approve.

❧ FOUR

From the time he could talk, Verne Fitch had no one to talk to, especially his parents. They were no longer young when he was born; he was a child conceived when all hope for a baby had been long abandoned.

"A true gift from God," May had said to Carl, the day they brought the baby home. "But my rightful due, I think. After all, I've always been a dedicated Christian and a loyal member of the church. God did not punish us just because you never went to services," she had said self-righteously.

Her dig did not go unnoticed. Carl simply ignored it, as he had so many other times. He was a simple quiet man who lumbered through life in a huge graceless body, but he was no fool. Now, cradling the new infant awkwardly in his arms, he smiled at the unexpected gift, and said softly, "Sure is a nice surprise."

"God has rewarded us."

"Sure, May, I guess I had nothin' to do with it." Hurt and angry, he handed the baby back to her and stomped off, unable to remember the last time they had intercourse. Maybe it had been an immaculate conception.

"You sure can cook, May," Carl said one night at dinner.

"You can thank my mother for that. She gave me a fine talking-to before we were married."

"Oh?" He tensed, wondering if a speech was coming on.

"Yes, be a good wife, she told me. Cook decent meals and keep the house neat and tidy."

"What else she tell you?" He knew what she would say, what she always said, but he asked her anyway. "About marriage, I mean."

"Oh, you know."

"Yeah." He poured himself another glass of milk. "Endure, right? That was her favorite word, endure. I'm not so stupid, May."

"Well, I did, didn't I? And now we have little Verne to show for it."

"You didn't endure me that much, May."

"It was enough, Carl. You know as well as I do that the day little Verne was born was my fortieth birthday. And now I have the right to say, enough!"

She picked up the dishes and stalked to the sink. "You take care of your work, and I'll take care of mine."

He glared at her stiff back, and said evenly, "You mean, I'll tend the farm and you raise the baby, right?"

"That's just what I mean, Carl."

He stared at her, the thin, small-boned body still bloated around the middle from pregnancy, and wondered if this drab colorless woman had ever been young, or pretty, or filled with the joy of life. He'd waited twenty years for her to change. He might as well wait twenty more, for all the good it did.

"You never did tell me nothin' about your trip to Chicago and Verne. How is he?" Carl asked. He and May sat at the kitchen table drinking warm milk. It was one a.m. on a cold Wednesday morning, and neither of them could sleep.

"Huh! You're suddenly interested. He's been gone four years."

"I know he's been gone four years. You'd think he'd have the decency to show up once in a while." His voice was querulous; she knew how to make him feel small. All she ever cared about was that boy. Buying him things they couldn't afford. May skimmed her hot milk with the back of a spoon. "He was here for Christmas. You never remember anything."

"I remember the two-dollar clothes brush he brought me. Made in HONG KONG." He made it sound like a disease.

"Everything with you is money," May said bitterly. "It was a beautiful thought. Imported, too." She grabbed her cup and walked to the sink, her worn slippers flip-flopping on the green linoleum. "Trouble with you is, you never really knew your son."

"Trouble with you is," Carl shot back in rare anger, "you never let me." His tired eyes were bloodshot, the lids drooping. "Can't you answer a simple question?"

May's shoulders sagged as she rinsed her cup. "He's okay."

"You spend one whole day in the big city and that's all you got to say about him? What's he doing? How does he pay the rent?"

She whirled around, her lips pursed and bloodless. "Money, money, money. There you go again. He hasn't asked you for any, has he?"

Carl ignored her, put his elbows on the table, which he knew she hated. "Where does he live?"

"A place called Uptown. A little apartment."

"He live alone? Or is he shacked up with some little painted tart?"

"Your mind runs in the gutter, you know that, Carl?"

"That's gutter talk to you. It ain't to me."

"Money and sex. I'm getting tired of hearing it."

"You wanna talk about God?" Now his voice was so low she could barely hear him, but the words made their impression. Her eyes glowed with inner fire, her body quivering in a sudden paroxysm of fervor. "How dare you blaspheme like that! I have seen HIM. I have talked with HIM!"

Carl stood and lumbered out of the kitchen. "Sure. And I just had tea with the Queen of England."

ϨϞ FIVE

The dirt hill behind Malden Street was growing higher every day as construction crews excavated for the new, exclusive housing development. One square block would become a series of attached homes. Gracing the center of the square would be a landscaped park with swimming pool and tennis courts. The houses would be two-story and trendy, to appeal to the newly rich young people working in Chicago. Gentrification, it was called. The older generation called it crazy; they had worked hard to move out of this neighborhood, their children now earning big bucks to move back in.

On Wednesday night the two little boys passed the NO TRESPASSING sign and began throwing a ball back and forth at the edge of the hill. This was their favorite place to play. They could slide down the hill, dig in piles of debris for imaginary treasure, and best of all, thumb their noses at the sign. At four o-clock, the workmen left and the equipment was chained, leaving them alone with no one to bother them. The lot, with rocks and deep ruts, was ill-suited for soccer or baseball, but these two loved it.

As one of the boys ran for the ball, he tripped on what he thought was a rock. He looked down to kick it out of the way.

It was not a rock. It was a shoe, low-heeled, tan leather, with stylish wing tips and brown laces. Intrigued, he called to his friend to come see what he had found. He began tugging at the shoe. When he finally pulled it free of dirt, he fell back, his eyes wide with horror.

Behind him, his friend, who had also glimpsed the leg that was attached to the foot that was inside the shoe, began to whimper. And then they both ran for help.

"We've got ourselves a corpse." Lieutenant Beltz hooked his fingers in his suspenders and sat back in his creaking chair.

"No shit? Missing a hand?" Jake Brankowsky asked.

"Yep."

"You think it's that woman been missing?"

"Don't know yet. Landlady can't make a positive I.D. 'til morning. Baby-sitting her niece. Goldberg's at the morgue."

Brankowsky grinned. "You can't rush Goldberg. But he'll have that corpse analyzed and catalogued before dawn."

"So far," Beltz added, "all he's told us is how long she's been dead, approximately seventy-two hours—she bought it some time Sunday night—death was caused by multiple stab wounds. Here, you want to see the glossies?"

He threw a large manila envelope on the desk.

Brankowsky opened it and flipped through the black and white pictures, all different angles, taken by the police photographer before the body was moved from the dirt hill.

The woman had been wearing blue jeans with a designer label and an outsized sweatshirt. Both were filthy and covered with dried blood. In spite of the blood and dirt, and the grotesque positions, Jake Brankowsky couldn't help thinking what a beautiful woman she must have been. Petite, doll-like, her blonde hair fanned out behind her like the spread of a peacock's tail. The handless arm looked phony, like a special effect, out of place on the lovely body. Glum-faced, Jake handed back the pictures to Beltz.

"By the way," he said, "did I see the Chief here the other night?"

"Yeah, I called him. Thought maybe he knew the missing woman. He knows the whole neighborhood."

"And...?"

"Claims he didn't know her."

"You believe him?"

"We can always find out."

"You trust him?"

"Have to. Do I have a choice?" Beltz looked at Jake quizzically. "Who'd you bring in?"

"Some old yahoo looking in a lady's window. She was stark naked but had enough brains to slam the window down on his fuckin' foot. We got him before he broke loose."

"Better his foot than something else."

Jake laughed and took the cigarette from behind his ear. He stuck it between his lips, unlighted.

"Thought you quit," Beltz chided.

"I did. Can't you tell? Doesn't count if you don't light it."

"How long has it been? Six months now?"

Jake frowned. "When did I break up with Carol? I guess six months. She never kept matches in the house. Or ash trays. I sort of got out of the habit. The only good thing she ever did for me."

"I don't know how you get along without a woman in the house," Beltz said, sitting upright. "Just keeping the place decent, and the laundry. I haven't found my socks since my wife died."

"Hell, Lieutenant, I don't need a woman for that," Jake said, making for the door.

Alone, Beltz thought about what he had just said. Socks weren't all he couldn't find. Sometimes he wondered if his sanity wasn't missing, too.

The phone rang. Beltz picked it up after the first ring. "Area Three, Beltz here. Yeah, Ziv...yeah...yeah...what?" His bushy eyebrows arched in surprise. "You making some kind of joke, Goldberg?"

He banged down the receiver and reached for his coat. As he ran out, he was heard mumbling something about the M.E.'s goofy sense of humor.

It was close to eleven o'clock at night when Molly started down Lawrence Avenue with her bag, poking around into several baskets along the street, pulling out a folding umbrella with bent spokes and a child's red plastic purse.

She tried to appear indifferent and not flinch when she touched dirty objects, especially if there were other vagrants nearby. Some were even hostile when she tried chatting with them earlier in the evening and she began to sense the competition for what could be salvaged and used or bartered for wine or smokes. She needed to find someone more cooperative, less threatened. Her bag-lady 101 course was too slow; at this rate, she might never graduate.

A wind kicked up and began blowing dirt and papers in swirling patterns near the gutters. Molly blinked against a bit of scratchy grit in one eye. It wouldn't budge. She turned against the shelter of a shop window and carefully pulled down her upper lid, working it around. But it still hurt.

"You need some help?" a high-pitched voice cracked.

Startled, Molly turned to see who had spoken. An old woman, dressed in the same natty elegance, looked at her questioningly.

"I have something in my eye," Molly said.

She should have known better.

It happened so fast she never saw the clenched fist pop out of the old woman's sleeve and aim straight for her chin. The blow hit Molly hard, knocking her against the glass window with such force she could no nothing but stare at her attacker as she slid down the smooth surface to the cement ground.

She saw the woman grin, her rotten protruding teeth like a jack-o-lantern. At the same moment Molly felt her bag ripped from her hands. She almost laughed. The old vulture should have picked someone else. Wait until she opens the bag and finds yesterday's Tribune, the torn purse, and the broken umbrella.

She wasn't sure how long she sat there on the cold sidewalk. It didn't surprise her that nobody stopped to ask about her health. When the squad car pulled to the curb, Molly, still woozy, let the policewoman help her up and into the back seat of the squadrol.

"I don't think she's hurt bad," the officer said to her partner, "but let's drop her off at the hospital to make sure."

"No—no hospital," Molly protested. "I feel okay."

"Yeah, well don't throw up back there. It was a mess last night and it's just been washed."

"I'm not drunk."

"She didn't smell drunk," the policewoman admitted. "She didn't smell at all. Strange?"

"Yeah," her partner said. "They usually reek. It works for them," he added, "keeps the others away."

"Let me out at the corner," Molly insisted, "I told you I feel fine."

"No, we'll take you to the station. You could use some hot coffee."

Molly panicked; if she went to the station, Detective Beltz might recognize her. And then the whole business of her masquerade, the hand and how she found it, would come out.

She also knew if she protested too much, her behavior might be suspect. She would say nothing. Hot coffee would taste good right now. She would drink it and get the hell out.

But Stanley Beltz was not around and Molly sighed with relief. She sat alone, huddled on a corner of the bench, watching a typical evening at Area Three Headquarters and drinking her coffee. Her rescuers had returned to the street leaving her utterly ignored. Amazing—how everyone looked right through her. She knew it was the clothes and the identity she had assumed, but it was demeaning.

31

Her jaw ached. She touched it tenderly and felt the swelling but knew it wasn't broken. By tomorrow morning she would look like she had gone three rounds with Mohammed something, or did he change his name. Who could keep up.

The room stopped spinning and she tried to stand. Every part of her body hurt. Maybe she would wait a few more minutes.

No sooner had she sat down than Beltz walked in and grabbed the phone on his desk. Molly tucked her face deeper into the army jacket collar and kept her eyes down. She heard every word he said.

"I'm looking for George Burning Tree...is he there? I thought this was his night at the Center...oh, the game's at Woodside? Can I call him there? Thanks."

"Hey, Lieutenant, I.D. that body yet?" the desk sergeant called.

"Not yet."

"How about calling the Indian Chief..."

"Yeah..." Beltz, while dialing, glanced at the huddled figure on the bench, stared briefly, then resumed his task.

"...as soon as you can get here, Chief. I think you'll know her. Yeah, I think you will."

Sergeant Neal spoke quietly to Beltz. Molly couldn't hear until the sergeant exclaimed, "No shit!" His surprise gave way to raucous laughter. "Seems like she lost more than her hand, huh?"

Molly tensed with excitement; they found it. They found the body.

She had to know more, but she couldn't very well go up and ask them. Someone else. She had to find someone else. This...Chief...the sergeant called him an Indian. He must know something.

One step at a time, slowly, careful not to draw attention to herself, Molly inched her way out of the station.

❧ SIX

Molly loved old buildings, and delighted in photographing extremes on the city horizon between the charming and the ultra modern. But the Chicago Indian Center was drab and devoid of any fancy brickwork. Its only advantage was its size, though it was dwarfed by big old mansions on both sides.

Molly walked into the Center Thursday morning, stopped, and stared at what had to be the antithesis of every set she had ever photographed. Three-legged chairs, torn and leaking overstuffed furniture, and wildly flocked red draperies between the reception room and the gym. It looked like prop heaven.

Molly found George Burning Tree sitting cross-legged on the gym floor. He was mending a basketball net and kept his eyes on his work when she entered.

"Mr. Burning Tree?"

George continued with his mending.

"You are Mr.Burning Tree. Or is it Mr. Tree?"

He looked up at her, waiting.

"I need a few minutes of your time."

"What for?"

She told him the same lie she told Beltz, then ventured unhesitatingly into the subject. "That girl...the one who was murdered?"

George said nothing.

"Did you know her?"

The expression in his black eyes and his stony silence should have warned her, but she was a novice playing a dangerous game, and like all novices, plunged recklessly ahead without heeding the danger signs.

"I hear you do good work at the Center and know a lot of people..."

"You're lying!" he blurted angrily. "You're writing a book. So why ask about a murder?"

"Well...it's all part of the plot." Her stomach knotted, but she persisted. "It did happen."

"That doesn't belong in your story." His voice was low and deep; he was the one clearly in control, which dismayed her.

"Okay, you're right." Molly sat on the floor, faced him, and crossed her legs. She watched him struggle with some loose ends of netting. "You should use the loop stitch there," she said patiently. "It holds better."

He paused. He was practical. He handed her the net. "Show me."

She took the net and began weaving the strands slowly between her fingers, looping the ends into a small knot. When she pulled, they held tight.

She handed it back.

He resumed the mending, using her new stitch. "You've done this before? Fixed basketball nets?"

Molly smiled. "I've worked with rope, Mr. Tree. Am I calling you by the right name?"

"George is okay. And your name, lady?"

"Fast. Molly Fast." She was amused by the gradual change in his personality. But she proceeded with caution. "Exactly what do you do here at the Center?" she asked.

"I work with about fifty kids. Always liked kids." He

shrugged. "Guess I'm good at it. My job is at Apollo Moving. They pay me there. I work here for nothing."

Molly had the feeling this was the longest conversation he'd had in years. She would keep to this path with him. Single file. "That's nice. A city project, or private funds?"

"Both. But the police help."

Molly leaned forward. "In what way?"

"The police wives raise money for equipment. But there's this one guy who started the whole thing. He pulled me in on a bum rap...you don't want to hear about all this."

"Oh, I do. Don't stop now."

"Beltz is a good guy...we got it all straightened out."

"Lieutenant Beltz? I know him." Molly's legs were stiff in this position, but she was reluctant to stand. If she did, he might stop talking. "He was helpful to me. Everyone's been great. In fact," she blurted, taking a chance, "it was going smoothly until the murder."

George looked up sharply from his mending. "Whose murder?"

"Oh, come on, George, you know. Everyone knows."

George grabbed Molly's arm, his thick fingers digging into her flesh with each word. "I don't know. You tell me."

"It's...just something I overheard at the police station. You're hurting my arm."

George stood suddenly, his movement swift and fluid and Molly was hardly aware of it. The net fell from his hands to the floor, but she didn't dare touch it.

"What else did you hear?" he demanded.

"Nothing," she said quickly, rising to her feet. "That's all I know."

Molly rubbed her arm where his fingerprints were clearly reddening on her skin. "I'd better leave," she said, flinging her bulky purse over one shoulder. "Thanks for your help."

She hoped he hadn't noticed how ill at ease she was or how carefully she was edging her way toward the door. The way he was standing, stolid, motionless, his body limned by the sun streaming in through the high windows, left her with the image of a cigar store Indian, frozen woodenly in time. She was damn glad he didn't have a tomahawk.

❧ SEVEN

Detective Stanley Beltz helped himself to three lumps of sugar from the ornate silver service Pearl Minkoff had placed on the coffee table. It was four o'clock Thursday afternoon.

"A cookie? Take a cookie. I baked them fresh today," Pearl urged.

He saw her hand trembling as she held out the plate and knew she was still upset from her earlier visit to the morgue. A nice old bird, he thought. Bright red hair, elegantly coiffed in an old-fashioned bubble that somehow seemed appropriate for her. A plump motherly woman who still cared about her looks.

As he sipped his tea, he glanced around the room, noting how every knick-knack had its own special spot on a shelf or table.

"I'm sorry you had to go through that ordeal this morning," he said.

"It was my first time. My last, I hope. I sure never thought she'd end up that way. Such a nice girl. Such a lady. That's rare today, you know. I have two other roomers, but Verna was always my favorite. She was always smiling, always ready to help me put my groceries away. Kind, you know?

Thoughtful. She even remembered my birthday last month with a lovely plant. Right there, behind you on that table. An African violet. Still blooming, see?"

Beltz glanced over his shoulder and smiled. "Then you liked her as a tenant."

"Oh yes. She never caused any problems. Neat as a pin. And quiet."

"Did she have friends?"

"Yes, a few." Pearl lowered her eyes. "Now I don't want you to get the wrong impression of Verna. But she did have a boyfriend. Visited her regularly."

"How regularly?"

"He came on Monday nights lately, sometimes on Thursdays. Well, I assumed it was the same man. It's only been the last few weeks that he's come on Thursdays too. I never saw him, but I heard Verna's door open. So they were together twice a week. It's not my business."

"Can you tell me about him?" Beltz asked.

"Well," Pearl began, warming to her subject, "he was a well-dressed gentleman, married, Verna told me, in his early forties, always wore a suit and tie. Not like the young men today — so casual. I assume he drove here, although I never saw his car. He must have parked away from the house. Of course he didn't know I saw him. I always ducked inside my apartment so I wouldn't embarrass him. I liked to imagine he was in the advertising business, an executive, you know, gray flannel suit and all."

She giggled. "He must have spent a lot of time under a sun lamp, always looking like he just came back from Florida. Tall, with neat grey hair, but he wasn't old, young-looking, as a matter of fact, with a gray mustache. Isn't that strange? So gray? With a young face?"

Beltz was writing in his little black notebook and glanced up. "Did he show this past Monday night?"

Pearl nodded. "Yes, mad as a wet hen."

"What did he say when you told him she wasn't here?"

"That's why he was so mad," Pearl explained. "I guess he was pretty used to those Monday nights. Anyway, he stalked out."

"Did Verna ever mention his name?"

"No, she didn't say much, outside of a few odds and ends, you know, about her private affairs." Pearl blushed a bright crimson. "What a play on words, huh?" She laughed. "Oh, I'm glad I can still laugh. I never thought I would again after this morning."

Beltz nodded sympathetically, then asked, "Did anyone else ever come to visit Verna? Girl-friends or family?"

"No girl-friends that I ever saw, and I don't know anything about her family."

"What about Sunday night? Did you see Verna?"

"No, I was gone for the day, visiting my daughter. I didn't get home until very late. And I went straight to bed."

"She never mentioned her plans for the day, anyone she was going to see?"

"No. We weren't that close. She had her life. I had mine."

Beltz sighed and closed his notebook. "Do you think I could see her room now?"

"Of course."

He followed Pearl Minkoff up the stairway, waited while she unlocked the door to Verna's apartment, and told her he'd see her downstairs later.

Once inside, Beltz felt he had suddenly walked into a scene from a French farce. There was draped satin and white lace everywhere, on the bed, at the window, around the little dressing-table. Mirrored trays on the dresser held a clutter of perfume bottles and dusting powder in fancy little boxes, a brass French phone on the bed stand, mirrors hanging from gold tasseled ropes attached to the ceiling molding. And not a picture on the walls.

The detective spotted a black portfolio leaning against a paint-spattered easel in the corner. He flipped through the pictures, cartoons and black ink caricatures, a few watercolors of landscapes and stormy seas. He knew enough about art to realize they were good, the artist talented, trained, skilled in form and color. Before leaving the room, he spied a charcoal sketch taped askew to the back of the bedroom door. He wandered into the tiny kitchen. On the counter was a Cuisinart and a white porcelain pitcher which held a myriad of cooking utensils including whisks of all sizes, a wooden lemon reamer, spoons and spatulas, all the accouterments of a gourmet cook.

He opened a cabinet near the sink and saw at least ten unopened boxes of rubber gloves. He shook his head. To keep her long nails nice, he supposed. He lingered a few minutes, then into the bathroom, inspecting the medicine chest, the under-sink cabinet holding hair sprays and hair dryers, liquids and creams for the face and body, a veritable warehouse of cosmetics. Why would such a young woman need all this stuff?

So far his inspection proved only that this was the home of an extremely feminine and vain woman who enjoyed cooking and painted extraordinarily well.

No matter how long he'd been a detective, going through someone's personal belongings always made him uncomfortable. He felt like an intruder. Handling their underclothes, their diaries and photographs, all the intimate objects the outside world was not privy to, made him feel like a thief in the night. He walked back into the bedroom.

This time he took in every detail of the room. Next to the double bed a pink cherub lamp perched on a night stand, the color of its shade matching the dainty painted dressing table. He stepped closer and fingered the tortoise-shell handles of the comb and brush. He could imagine her sitting, looking in the mirror, pulling the brush through her long blonde hair.

An envelope was tucked under the brush. It was empty, but had a return address on the back: M. Fitch, R.R. #5, Fort Wayne, Indiana 46813. Odd. It was addressed to Verne Fitch at a P.O. number in Chicago. He pulled a plastic bag from his pocket, lifted the envelope carefully with his handkerchief, and dropped it into the bag.

He moved to the dresser. A small jewelry box in the top drawer contained several gold and silver rings of little value, a few pairs of dangling earrings, and a strand of cheap imitation pearls. Then he saw the bracelet.

Silver links with a band in the center. He took it to the window. On the top of the band, the name Verna was engraved. He turned it over. An inscription read: Without Indiscretion – Bob 9/22/95.

Without indiscretion. He had heard that before. But where? It began nagging at him. He ran fingers through his thick hair and wondered why, when you pass fifty, you suddenly can't remember anything.

He knew that phrase. Damn it. He could see it on a printed page. Now if he could just remember from where.

❧ EIGHT

When the Art Institute inaugurated a new student show in their lovely garden last year, Ellie Markham, co-owner of the prestigious Markham Gallery, made a point of attending. She was anxious to see what the graduating class had to offer. She literally stumbled over Verne Fitch's work.

Ellie had been meandering her way through the easels set up on the flagstone terrace, wearing high heels instead of her usual flats. A tall big-boned woman still affecting a low-heeled preppie look from college days, she looked almost fashionable in her new blue silk dress and matching high-heeled shoes. Even the new barrette holding one side of her straight brown hair was blue.

Intent on the rows and rows of paintings, she was tripped up by a small rise in the flagstones. As she started to fall, knocking over an easel on her way down, a small young man grabbed her arm to steady her, no mean feat considering the disparity in their size.

"Oh…I'm so sorry," Ellie cried, "the painting…it isn't damaged, is it?"

"Not the slightest," Verne Fitch said gallantly, placing his watercolor landscape back on the easel.

"Yours?" she asked.

"Yes." His voice was shy, soft.

Ellie stepped back and studied his paintings. "Is this the only medium you work in?"

"I like watercolors," he explained. "They seem to work for me, but I do a lot of pen and ink sketching, caricatures mostly. I used to quick-sketch in charcoal, but I haven't for years."

"Oh, I'm being rude. Let me introduce myself. Ellie Markham."

"From Markham Galleries?" Verne asked, shaking hands.

"You've heard of us?"

"We all have. You've helped quite a few no-names get started. That's very encouraging." Verne gazed steadily at Ellie, almost without blinking.

She stared back, transfixed by his luminous eyes. They were the lightest gray she had ever seen, with an almost silvery cast and an upward slant at the outer edges. Strange, compelling eyes, and she was willing to hover in the moment.

"I like your painting. How much is it?" A raspy voiced fat man had broken the silence as he pointed to Verne's landscape.

"Sorry, it's not for sale," Verne said politely.

The fat man moved away, grumbling, and Ellie, puzzled, said, "Why did you say that? Am I looking at something that's already sold?"

Verne smiled. The dappled sunlight through the blossoms of a crab-apple tree glinted on his short blond hair. A Botticelli cherub, Ellie said to herself, thinking, as she usually did, in artistic terms.

"I don't like to play games," Verne said, shrugging. "You were here first."

"And you hoped I would buy it." She was amused. "What if I walk away right now, tell you I was only looking. You'd have no sale at all."

"I took a chance."

"You sure did, because I'm very selective."

"I'm counting on that."

The conversation was unsettling. Ellie was accustomed to straight-forward business deals. This kid was tip-toeing around, playing his own kind of game. But damn it, he could paint.

"You mentioned caricatures," Ellie said bluntly, "can I see them?"

"They're not here. A secret vice, I guess, but I keep them at home."

"I would like to see them." The fat man stood a few feet away, eavesdropping. "And," she continued, "I'll take the watercolor."

As if expecting this transaction, Verne handed her the landscape. "I'll bring the sketches to the gallery."

She gave him a check, tucked the painting under her arm, and said, "I'll see you there tomorrow. Two o-clock sharp."

Verne watched Ellie teeter away on her high heels and thought about his mother. She walked that same way dressed up for church. It was her favorite place. When he showed little interest in toys, she would tell him New Testament stories, working at her chores, punctuating tales of the disciples or passions of prophets with a snap of the sheets or the swish of the mop. Withdrawing into a world of his own, Little Verne shut out friends and teachers and day-dreamed his way through school.

"Pay attention, Verne," his teachers in the lower grades would say. By seventh grade they were at their wits' end.

"Verne Fitch!" one called out, startling him. "Don't play-act with me, pretending to look at the blackboard while your fingers are sneaking around with the pencil. I see you all right, drawing those ridiculous pictures. You'll come to no account for sure if you don't start paying me some mind. Now bring me those pictures. They belong in the trash!"

In his high school freshman year, Mrs. Ryan, his math teacher, found his foolscap notebook under his desk after class, and took time to look through the pages of drawings.

The next day she took him aside.

"Verne, these are wonderful. The caricatures are so clever, even this one of me." She smiled, pointing to a sketch of herself standing in front of the class. "Is my nose really that long? Well, if it looks that way to you, I guess it is. You have a wonderful talent, Verne. I would suggest art courses next semester to perfect your skills. A solid technique will enhance your talents, and if you can draw cartoons, you can learn to draw other things as well. Go to it, my boy."

Two important events occurred in his sophomore year. Tom Carpenter died, and little Verne found a reason to live. Although both events were unrelated, they changed the shape of his life forever.

After years of childhood loneliness, he had finally found a friend, someone to share ideas with, thoughts, laughter and dreams. Tom and little Verne were best friends since their first day of high school. It was an unlikely twosome.

Tom was handsome and popular, a big farm boy who found it easy to flirt with the girls and be one of the boys. Little Verne admired Tom's popularity and upbeat personality, and Tom saw in little Verne a gentle, sensitive friend, a good listener who would laugh at his jokes and feel keenly his disappointments. Their close relationship flourished until the day Tom fell under the steel teeth of a soil cultivator.

In deep depression, little Verne remained in his room for five days. When he finally emerged, he walked into the kitchen and announced to his parents that from this day forward they were never to call him little Verne. His name was Verne, and he repeated what Tom had told him once: "Don't let anybody call you little anything. When you say little, you think little, and you ain't little."

The other event that year was his art exhibit in the school gymnasium on parents' night. In only a few months, under the guidance of his art teacher, Verne's doodles had blossomed from scribblings to witty pen and ink caricatures of faculty and students.

"Mrs. Fitch, you must be so proud of your son," the art teacher told May that night. "Verne certainly has the gift of catching those subtle peculiarities we all have. He has such a bright future."

Every free moment was time to sketch, and as he improved, he ventured into landscapes and still lifes. His sorrow over Tom was eased by the work load he imposed upon himself, and the memory of his friend remained fresh and alive. When he received notice of a scholarship to the Art Institute in Chicago, he only wished Tom could have shared his joy.

Verne Fitch showed up at the Markham Gallery the following day. This was the break he had dreamed of, to be discovered, given the chance to sign an exclusive contract with an important dealer. If it worked out, his career was set.

And it was possible. You had to have a goal. Dancers dreamed of big Broadway musicals, sopranos aim for the Met. Why not shoot for the Guggenheim...

His daydream took off, the docent just about to introduce his exhibition, when Ellie opened the door.

"You're very prompt," she said.

"One of my vices." Verne half-smiled and followed her into the living room. His eyes took in everything, the white upholstery and carpeting, the mix of antiques and glass cubes. He was pleased with himself, choosing to wear good slacks and jacket. Looking like a poor artist went just so far.

"It's too bad my husband is out. He was quite impressed with your painting and eager to meet you. Perhaps another time."

Verne stood at the window. "Yes," he said absently, absorbed with the astonishing view. "I'd like to paint *that* some day."

She had walked soundlessly to his side. "It's always this way. So much going on...the park, joggers, bikers, tennis, and the boats, of course. They all seem to materialize on the first warm day."

"Fabulous."

"Well, may I see what you brought?" Ellie said abruptly.

Verne opened his portfolio and began spreading out ink sketches on the square glass coffee table. At once, John Lennon and Princess Grace, Henry Kissinger and Dolly Parton sprang to life from the table top.

"Dear boy," Ellie gushed, "these are marvelous. Certainly not like those dreadful quick-sketches done at art fairs. They are well thought-out, insightful drawings. It's remarkable how you've captured those expressions with only a few pen lines. I know it's not smart business to be so enthusiastic, but I have to be honest with you. I don't like pretense. You're good, and I'll tell you so."

Verne's heart thumped in his chest, his hands icy cold. He had finally heard words only dreamed of. No more Walter Mitty fantasies. Here was somebody telling him a fact he already knew, but until this moment, had never been confirmed. He felt like jumping up and down and shouting, "Yeeoww!" Instead, he said calmly, "I'm pleased you like them."

His gray eyes were even more compelling today, and Ellie did her best to avoid them. He was only a boy.

"I want you to look over this contract, Verne, and when you're satisfied with the wording, you can sign. It's an exclusive with the Markham Gallery."

"I don't have to read it. I trust you."

"No, please look at it. I don't want any misunderstanding."

Verne read through quickly and signed. He looked at her, his gaze cool, opaque. "I'm grateful to you, Mrs. Markham. You'll always be very special to me."

Ellie felt the heat and color rising in her face and turned aside. "That's sweet, Verne. I know this will be a profitable relationship for both of us." She extended her hand. "Thank you for coming. I'll see you to the door."

"Am I being dismissed?"

"We've concluded our business."

Ellie had suddenly turned stiff and unfriendly. He wouldn't push it.

"Right. But remember, Mrs. Markham, one day soon I want to paint that scene from your window. Promise?"

She walked him to the door. "We'll see you very soon. I can't wait for you to meet my husband."

❧ NINE

Molly switched off the Channel 2 nightly news and thought irritably, what do you have to do in this town to make the news when you're murdered? Be a mafia don stuffed in a car trunk?

She could go through the morning paper again, for she was more than curious…finding that hand bound her forever to the ugly intrusion in her life.

Retrieving the Thursday morning Tribune from the waste basket, she began riffling through the front section. Nothing.The Tempo pages included articles about theatre and movies and advice to the sick and lovelorn. No point in even looking through the food section. And mergers and grain futures in Business were no help.

It was in the Chicagoland section that a local item on the bottom of page three stopped her cold.

MUTILATED CORPSE FOUND IN UPTOWN.

The story was only one paragraph. The who, what, when, and where, but of course, no why. It read:

"A woman's body was discovered Wednesday night in the dump site of the newly excavated Malden Street Mews development, according to police. The body was clothed, and police had, with the help of neighbors, made an iden-tification, said Lieutenant Stanley Beltz of the Area Three Violent Crimes Division. He said it appeared the woman, Verna Lake, 24, had been dead for several days. The body was taken to the Cook County medical examiner's office, where an autopsy will be performed Thursday, Beltz said. The left hand of the body, found earlier, had been severed."

Found earlier is right, Molly thought grimly, by me. Poor girl. Someone who had laughed and cried and lived and breathed. Now just a body without a hand.

Maybe it was becoming an obsession, but she was irrevo-cably involved. Sky always said she was tenacious. She pre-ferred to think of it as persevering. Either way, there was no letting go.

She reached for the phone book and turned to the L's.

"They're still blooming?" Molly leaned over the fence at 418 Kenmore Avenue and pointed to the rose bush Pearl was pruning.

Pearl Minkoff looked up, a chunky figure in a gardening smock and oversize work gloves, and smiled at the compli-ment to her dear roses.

"Well, I give them loads of attention and they pay me back. Sort of like your children. We should be so lucky."

Pearl chatted amiably with the woman. "I know a city gar-den is rare these days, but we have so much sun. Otherwise, all you get is green — no flowers."

"You must be an expert, judging from those beautiful blooms."

"I guess I am. But only because I've been doing it so long."

Pearl straightened up, gathered basket and rose shears, and began walking toward the house.

"Excuse me," Molly called, "are you Mrs. Lake?"

Pearl turned. "Mrs. Lake?"

"This is where Verna Lake lives, isn't it?"

"Well...yes, but...who are you?" Pearl bristled. "Are you a reporter? I've had them here all morning. I've said all I'm going to say."

She turned abruptly and walked up the front steps.

"Oh, no—no—no, I'm not a reporter. I found Verna's purse on the subway...and I wanted to return it. It had her name and address in it. See?"

Pearl stopped on the top step, turned, and looked at Molly, trying to assess the woman's story. "Verna's purse? Maybe you don't know what happened to Verna?"

"No. Tell me," Molly said innocently.

"She died. About five days ago."

"Oh, Mrs. Lake, I'm so sorry."

"Lady, I don't know who *you* are, but I know I'm not Mrs. Lake."

"You're not?"

"No. This is my house, and Verna lived here." Pearl started back down the stairs. "Now, if you want to give me the purse, I'll be glad to put it with her other things."

Molly's charade crumbled. "Do you think I could come in and talk to you for a few minutes?"

"What about?"

"About Verna. It's terribly important."

Pearl hesitated. But the woman seemed sincere and was obviously distressed. And maybe Pearl could learn something more about Verna and help the police. And maybe that nice detective would come again for tea.

"Well, all right. But just for a few minutes."

Molly followed Pearl into the house and took a seat on the sofa in the front room. Pearl plumped herself into an easy chair and looked at Molly over the top of her glasses.

"So, tell me what's so important?"

"Mrs. ...Mrs?"

"It's Minkoff. Mrs. Pearl Minkoff."

"Mrs. Minkoff. You've been so kind to let me into your home, I must be honest with you."

51

Molly went on to explain the whole grisly business of finding the hand, what she had been doing there in the first place, and how she finally discovered that the hand belonged to Verna.

"So why do you want to become involved in this? Let the police take care of it. That's their job."

"Yes, but don't you see," Molly said gravely, "I simply have to know. You must understand...I had that poor girl's hand in my lap!"

"Oh dear," Pearl said softly.

"Can you help me? Will you help me?"

Pearl sighed heavily. "What can I do?"

"Tell me about Verna."

Pearl repeated to Molly everything she had already told Lieutenant Beltz. The more she talked, the more she remembered, and it was over an hour later when she finally finished her narrative.

The sun had disappeared during this time and the room had darkened. Molly could see the lines of age etched deep in Pearl's face and was almost sorry she had put her through this.

"I'd better go," she said.

"No," Pearl protested, "let me make some tea. And I have some delicious cookies."

While Pearl fussed in the kitchen, Molly mulled over what she had just heard. The girl's loose way of life seemed to have been accepted by this old-fashioned, straight-laced woman. What about the man in Verna's life. A business man? An attorney? A doctor? Maybe a car dealer. They can dress nice, too. And what about her family? Don't they know? Don't they care? Why haven't they shown up. Odd. If somebody's child...

"Here we are," Pearl said, coming in from the kitchen. "Some nice hot tea and my very special butternut cookies."

"Do women still bake?"

"Well, I bake most every day even for myself. It's cheery and civilized and it reminds me of how things used to be.

"You see, when Sam and I moved here, this was a nice middle-class neighborhood. We took care of our houses, we all knew each other on the block, we'd sit outside in the summer and talk to our neighbors. Some of the men had poker clubs, and the ladies would go shopping downtown together. That all changed a while back, you know? Different people started moving in. Like when the Solomons sold their home and moved to Miami, then it was all downhill. Strangers came. Hill people, how do you say? Hillbillies, Orientals, Indians, big families in small apartments, and not even families...just lots of people crowding in together."

Molly was polite, but her thoughts were on the murder, the hand, the ring.

"The ring!" she blurted, "the snake ring! What about the snake ring?"

Pearl sat down, the tray teetering dangerously on her lap. "You mean Verna's gold ring?"

"Yes. Do you know anything about it? Who gave it to her?"

Pearl thought for a moment. "Gold, right? With green eyes, emeralds, I think. It looked expensive. I never saw it until they showed it to me at the morgue. I thought it was ghastly myself. I hate snakes."

"But the ring," Molly interrupted, "do you think they were real stones?"

"Oh they were real, all right."

"I wish we knew more about that man you mentioned. Maybe he gave it to her."

Pearl Minkoff swallowed hard. "Do you think so?"

"It is a clue."

The older woman put the tray on the table and began pouring tea. "Wait a minute!" Pearl looked up. "I just thought of something. When you mentioned the ring..."

"Go on," Molly urged.

"There was another piece of jewelry...a bracelet. Maybe it was given to her by the same man. She never told me."

"What did it look like?"

53

"It was…wait! I have the receipt from the detective right here in the desk. He found it in her jewelry box and took it for evidence, I think. Anyway, the receipt has a description on it."

Pearl jumped up, knocking over her cup, and hurried to her desk. "Here it is. I left my glasses in the kitchen. What does it say?"

Molly took the paper and read out loud: "One silver bracelet, links, with inscribed band in center — Verna, topside, 'Without Indiscretion'—Bob on the back and a date — 9/22/95 — sterling hallmark. It's signed S. Beltz, Lieutenant, Area Three, Violent Crimes."

The two women looked at each other.

"He's got it? The detective, I mean?" Molly asked.

"Yes. He took it with him yesterday." Pearl was puzzled. "Why? Is this important?"

"If it ties in with the ring, it could be."

"Don't you think the police are investigating that?" Pearl said.

"Sure. With all the big jewelers in town."

"I know what you're thinking," Pearl said slyly, "maybe it was bought from one of the little guys, the neighborhood shops. Like my Sam. Out of the way. So it would be hard to find. The gangsters liked that when they bought fur coats for their…"

"Exactly. You said he was a married man. Verna told you that. And he wouldn't want to be recognized. He'd stay away from the Michigan Avenue shops. Chances are, if he's fooling around, around here, then he doesn't live around here, then he's safe in buying it around here. Right?"

Excitement caused Molly's words to tumble out faster than she could think. "I have to be going. You've given me so much of your time, and I appreciate it."

"Not at all. And take some cookies with you. But I still say you'd better be careful. There's a murderer out there, and you've had no experience with that. If you get into trouble, you can't even defend yourself." Pearl shook her head. "*I* wouldn't get involved."

"*You* didn't find the hand, Mrs. Minkoff."

❧ TEN

Lieutenant Stanley Beltz and medical examiner Ziv Goldberg sat at a corner booth in Grady's Tavern nursing their second beers. They always preferred the booth for its privacy; they also liked the fact that it was next to the kitchen. That way their orders were quickly whisked to the table, and the risk of returning to work hungry if their beepers went off was greatly diminished. Grady's was one of the last of the neighborhood taverns. So many of the city's residential streets were torn up and rehabbed, which increased the value of the land and sent taxes to the moon, and without sufficient clout, some of the owners saw the old rickety structures coming down.

The Grady family still owned the tavern, plastering the four walls with photographs of Chicago's political elite, a pictorial chronicle of Mayor Daley's rise to power, candid shots with governors and state senators, the rich Irish and the religious who backed him financially, and the young Irish senator from Massachusetts who went on, with Daley's help, to become President of the United States. Just this past April, the new Mayor Daley was placed proudly beside the old. Jure divino.

Beltz had telephoned Ziv that Friday morning to meet him for lunch at noon. Ziv readily agreed. It got him away from the morgue's grim basement for a couple of hours. And he did love Grady's lean corned beef.

Ziv had spent half the night on an autopsy, a ward committeeman whose body had been found floating in his sunken car off the 55th Street beach. By dawn he had managed a few hours of uneasy sleep on the couch in his office. Now, he needed a shave.

"I was shocked," Ziv said, as they talked about the Verna Lake case, "I'll admit it. I've been a doctor for a lot of years, seen a lot of weird homicides, opened more than a few corpses done in for some odd-ball reasons, but this one takes the prize."

"Yeah, but I still don't understand," Beltz said, "how any guy can do that to himself."

"Stan, look at it this way. This kid obviously had a horrendous problem. It must have been destroying his life."

"It did," Beltz observed wryly.

"But not of his own choosing, that's the difference."

Ziv looked up at Beltz, his watery blue eyes tired behind rimless bifocals. A balding, stern, professorial type, Ziv liked nothing better than to expound on his own pet theories. He had a lot of them, dealing mostly with the psychological implications of a crime rather than the forensic results. And Beltz was a good listener. Maybe it was his profound respect for the M.E.'s knowledge, or his insatiable curiosity about all aspects of a case, but either way, he made a perfect audience.

"I'm sure," Ziv continued, "he tried to alleviate his emotional trauma with this drastic solution."

"Drastic is right. It hurts me just to think about it." The lieutenant belched and looked straight at the medical examiner. "Jesus, who in his right mind would have his pecker cut off!"

Ziv took a swallow of beer. "Don't assume this was a snap decision on his part. He must have gone through the tortures of hell. Think about it. Psychiatric evaluation, hormones, estrogen implants. He didn't just walk in off the street and ask some surgeon to turn him into a woman on a whim." Ziv made wet circles with his glass on the heavy oak table top, and said thickly, "The pain must have been grotesque."

Beltz shook his head. "I don't get it."

"You don't have to get it. It's a fact. You saw it. I saw it. That pretty little blonde was once somebody's son. Verna was once Pete or Frank or Joe."

"Tell me, Ziv, why would he do it?"

"They're all kinds of reasons. A domineering mother, a weak mother, a weak father or a tyrant, or none at all, a kid who likes to dress in his sister's clothes...a bad errant gene or a childhood experience so ugly it twisted his sexual identity...take your pick, it could be any of those. Or none. We'll never know with Verna. She's dead."

Beltz wiped some foam from his upper lip. "The family's got to turn up. We're checking, plus any doctors he saw, the school, friends, people living in the Minkoff house. The apartment turned up zilch. Apparently he...she...Christ!...broke off all friendships when she had the operation."

The waitress set their corned beef sandwiches on the table with a smile for the two men. Familiar customers are good tippers, especially old cops. The young ones were cheap.Probably figured the thrill of waiting on them was enough. Ziv rubbed his hands together in glee before digging in.

Beltz bent back one edge of the rye bread and moaned. "So lean. Too lean. Where's the fat corned beef these days?

"This is better, Stan, better for your heart, and your cholesterol, and your..."

"Ah, nuts. You and your fancy new diets. One day you guys will be touting cigarettes and chocolate sundaes. What is it, every twenty-five years that trends get reversed?"

His mouth already full, Ziv waved at Beltz's sandwich. "Eat, eat," he said.

They chewed in silence. The waitress brought another two beers and removed the empties.

"Ziv, what about her hand? Why would the killer cut off her hand?"

The medical examiner, still chewing, looked up and said, "Beats me. All I can tell you is no surgeon did that. It was hacked at, repeatedly, until it finally came off. But you know, Stan, that isn't what killed her. Those stab wounds…so many and so crazy…so vicious…hell, you saw the body."

Beltz poured fresh beer into his glass and washed down the huge bite he had taken. "Which one killed her?"

"The first two, as a matter of fact, the ones in her back. Lacerated the aorta. She must have died instantly. The others were pure pleasure."

"Pleasure?"

"Sure, pleasure for the killer. Or monstrous rage. Haven't had a corpse with the breasts sliced off like that in a long time."

"Something I have to ask, Ziv. How could she fool the guys she slept with?"

Ziv drained his glass and said, "It was a good job. They take the penile skin and fashion it into a vagina. It works because of the tactile sensitivity. No orgasms, but with them it doesn't matter. It's the physical closeness they're after. Anyway, lots of women fake it."

"Mm-mm." Beltz chewed thoughtfully for a minute. "And a guy really can't tell the difference? Amazing. I wonder if I was ever fooled in my younger days."

"No, Stan," Ziv said, his somber face creasing into a smile, "when you were messing around, this surgical procedure was rare. And don't forget how the hand fooled you. When you first saw it, you were sure it was a woman's hand, remember?"

"Did you know?"

"Not until I ran the tests. And by then, we had the body. Bizarre case, Stanley."

Goldberg reached into his inside jacket pocket, withdrew a forensic report, and handed it to Beltz. "Here it is, the results of the spectrographic analysis. Residue of charcoal dust under the fingernails. That's about all we found. Except of course the ring. And the clothes."

"Charcoal dust? Coal? Or a barbecue?"

"No. It was structured, woody, from sticks of charcoal, you know, the kind artists use."

Beltz paid the check, left a good tip for the smiling waitress, and walked out into the bright October afternoon with Ziv.

"Thank you, Stanley, that was a treat indeed."

"I still say it was too lean. It's the fat that…"

"Makes you fat, Stanley. Listen to me." Beltz declined a ride back to headquarters and began slowly walking the narrow quiet streets. Chicago was a city of neighborhoods, ethnic enclaves where the small frame houses and bungalows on narrow lots reflected lifetimes of savings and hard work. Where owners stood fast against encroaching decay, the properties were neat and carefully tended. Big old trees arched over the one-way streets and the line of homes continued unbroken except for the occasional mom and pop grocery on the corner.

Beltz had been raised in such a neighborhood, not far from where he now walked. But there the decay had found an entrance, working itself in when families fled blight and change. He thought grimly of his old house, now a six-flat building housing an ethnic mix that would have defied even a U N peace mission. He rarely walked that street now.

He sidestepped a broken section of sidewalk. Verna Lake's life had ended like that, he thought. Whatever family she had must be as ruined and fractured as the broken pieces of cement he now kicked into the gutter. Who were they? What upheaval had they suffered when their son underwent his physical transformation? Did they know who he became afterwards? Did they care?

Beltz had been dead serious when he had asked Ziv all those questions at lunch, and had been seeking real answers. It wasn't the actual physical mutilation, but rather the grinding emotional turmoil the boy must have suffered that disturbed him. And now the girl who had once been a boy was dead, and no one was mourning. All the pain had been for nothing.

Bizarre, Ziv had said, but it was more than that. It was lunacy. And try as he did, Beltz could not understand it. He had lived for fifty-six years in what Sandburg had called the city of the big shoulders, hog butcher to the world. He had watched the stockyards die and gangs born, and now it was choking on drugs and violence and crime. As Sandburg had also said, while the singers sang and the strong men listened, there were rats and lizards also listening...and the only listeners left now are the rats and lizards.

Beltz shuddered and walked faster. Men becoming women,women becoming men, and this is the middle of the country, for God's sake, not one of the crazy coasts where maybe things like that happen every day.

A cheerful man by nature, he didn't relish these joyless ruminations. And he was still no closer to any answers. Except one. From his point of view, sex was just fine the way it was.

⅔ ELEVEN

When Bob and Ellie Markham remodeled three rooms of their Lakeview apartment into their chic little gallery, the project was unique, and Ellie, a former assistant curator at the Museum of Modern Art in New York, was delighted.

"I'll finally have a chance to use my knowledge," Ellie gushed to her husband. "They never gave me the position I deserved in New York. I was underpaid, underutilized, and over-qualified. This situation is perfect. But we'll have to move carefully…look for the exceptional…show works that will make our collection different."

Ellie was successful at giving the impression of old eastern social status and wealth. Delighting in telling of her long line of eminent ancestors, she expounded on an involved saga of her father's immigration. "One of the young European aristocrats sailing to the New World in search of his fortune," she would trill proudly. She had told it so often, in time she came to believe it. Actually, he had stowed his way across the sea, miserably sick, from Rumania.

But the man was clever, worked hard, and made smart land buys in Baltimore. His estate and gentleman's manners soon opened doors of the socially prominent, allowing Ellie to move only in the best circles. Which is how she met the old-moneyed Markhams, and Bob. Ellie preferred her husband's lineage to her own.

They shared the collection responsibilities, but it was Ellie who negotiated price with the artists. It was her style to look like she never had a dime, while Bob, with his corporate image and fastidious dress, she pointed out more than once, could easily lead the artist to demand more.

On this Friday afternoon, Bob had just completed the largest sale the gallery had ever made to The Jonathon DeVries Architectural firm, their corporate offices buying eight canvases. He should have been elated, but his fingers holding the check were clammy and trembling. His temples throbbed and his mouth tasted sour.

Since reading the item in the paper about the murdered woman in Uptown, Bob's upwardly mobile life had suddenly ground to a halt. He had been stupid, there was no doubt of that, getting involved as deeply as he had with that girl. He blamed Ellie, not himself, for his infidelity. Had she needed him more, been more receptive, more feminine, he might not have turned to Verna in the first place. But at the time he hadn't realized how much he'd been missing good sex.

And Verna was an expert. She made him feel like a man. "C'mon, my sweet," she purred, "I'll take you to the stars. I'll take you to points of pleasure you've never even dreamed of. We'll soar together, just you and me." Hell, she gave him back his balls.

With Verna, he'd stepped out of his skin to watch. He was a voyeur at his own performances. Maybe that's what had made it so exciting, so kinky. Fuck Prissy Ellie and her eastern girls-school approach to life. She may know the art world, but she knows zilch about screwing.

Bob walked to the windows and looked out at the darkening sky over the lake, absently wringing his hands. During the past twenty-four hours he had gone over and over every detail of his hours with Verna. He'd been cautious, parking blocks away on Monday nights so the nosy landlady couldn't see his car. Hell, Verna never even knew his last name. There wasn't anything to connect Bob Markham to the dead woman.

The unlit room was chilly, but beads of perspiration broke out on his forehead, and he loosened his tie. The bracelet. That God-damn bracelet she'd wanted so much. "Bob, angel, it would be a tender part of you always next to me. It would be so special. Please. Please. Please!" And so he bought it. But he needn't worry about that. He had paid cash. Anyway, the inscription wouldn't mean a thing to anyone else. And there must be a zillion Bobs in this world. And they'd never trace it to that crummy little shop. He poured a stiff shot of scotch and downed it in one gulp. It was a relief, now that she was gone. Lately Verna had been like one of those deadly female spiders who spin a web around their mate until the poor boob dies, and he feared more than anything being caught in a web of any kind. Imprisoned, controlled, that was not what he'd had in mind when negotiating their first carnal transaction.

She had done things to him he'd only seen in porno films, and the more she invented, the tighter he was hooked. Wild improvisational sex that had released in him an animal he barely recognized. The straight-arrow, well-manicured gentleman evaporated the minute he slipped between her satin sheets. The new fellow was more exciting, and certainly a lot more fun. He'll miss him, but he can live without him.

Bob flipped on the lamp near the bar and poured another scotch. The amber liquid spilled over the edge of the glass as he tossed it down, and he wiped his fingers on a fussy embroidered bar cloth Ellie had picked up in Rome.

A tanker far in the distance moving north on the lake caught his eye. In only a few moments the ship would disappear from sight. No wake, no smoke, nothing left to indicate it had ever been there. If he had been as prudent as he hoped, he'd be in the same boat.

Molly had made a list of neighborhood jewelry stores gathered from the yellow pages, but the whole idea was incongruous. If the poor were flush, trinkets were the most unlikely things they'd buy. You can't eat a gold necklace. Maybe that's why the list was so small.

Luckily the Uptown area was inside the border of Irving Park on the south, Foster on the north, and Ravenswood on the west. East of Sheridan Road your hat would float. So the search was manageable.

Although it was late Friday afternoon, Molly set out to visit as many shops as she could before they closed. The first one was shuttered due to a death in the family. The second in the same block only sold cheap costume jewelry. The proprietors of the next three were patient, listened to her description of the silver bracelet, but never handled anything similar in their stores.

She checked those off her list and headed for Baubles, Bangles, and Beads on north Clark Street. It was five-twenty, and the owner was just pulling the iron gate across the front entrance.

"Come back tomorrow," he told Molly, "we'll still be here."

"Your sign says you close at five-thirty," she said indignantly, "I only need a minute."

"What are you looking for, lady?"

"A silver bracelet, the kind with links, like an identification bracelet."

He left the gate half open and pointed toward the window display. "Like that?"

Molly saw a group of I.D. bracelets of varying sizes off to one side, dusty and neglected.

"We don't get much call for those anymore, but silver still costs me plenty," he added quickly.

Innocently, Molly asked, "Have you sold any recently?"

"Not since June. Graduation time, you know. They make nice gifts for special occasions."

That was that. "I'm sure they do. Maybe I'll think of something else. I'll come back tomorrow."

He shrugged and closed the gate.

Molly checked that shop off her list. With the date September 22 on the back, the bracelet wasn't bought here.

She glanced at her watch. All the stores would be closed by now. Why is it only in the movies that detectives get answers so quickly, she wondered. This is damn hard work.

At nine the next morning, Molly was standing on Clark in front of Nick's Uptown Jewelers — Estates Bought and Sold. She couldn't miss the torn awning and the window dressing looking as though watches, rings, earrings, and pendants had been dropped willy-nilly on a bed of faded green velvet like a hastily tossed salad. But there were several silver link bracelets.

As she entered the shop, a little bell tinkled over the door. The owner, a rotund elf, was behind the counter peering through a loupe at the inside of a watch.

"You'll have to wait," he called, "these quartz jobs are a pain in the ass."

"Take your time. I'll look around," Molly said.

The shop was long and narrow, the walls lined with rickety shelves straining at their nails from the weight of odd and eclectic junk. Paintings were stacked on the floor. Brass spittoons, old copper pots, an ornate silver samovar and a scarred school desk were but a few of the items crowded in between the showcases. Looking down on all of this was a suit of armor hanging precariously from the ceiling on shredded drapery cords. Instinctively, Molly stepped back.

"Now then, what can I show you?" the little man asked.

"I'm looking for a silver bracelet. An I.D. bracelet. The kind you can engrave."

"We have some."

"Yes, I saw them in the window. Are they good sellers?" Molly asked.

"Hm-mm, so-so," Nick said, gesturing palm up, palm down. "You want any special one from the window?"

"No. Bring a few out and I'll look. Can you engrave anything I want on it?"

"Sure. As long as it isn't dirty. I won't do that." He chuckled and placed four bracelets on the counter.

She examined them as though interested in buying. "Has anybody ever asked you to do that?"

"Yes, but they had to clean it up." His beady little eyes twinkled.

"I bet people ask for all sorts of things. Undying love or...a quote from Shakespeare..."

"I've had some funny ones. Weird ones too. Like once this lady had me engrave, `to my Shotsie—from his mommy.' And you know who was wearing it? She came in one day and would you believe? That bracelet was around her itty-bitty doggie's neck."

Molly laughed.

"And there was another one," he went on, "and I don't have to understand them, mind you, some of 'em are in a foreign language, and this one might as well have been."

Molly shifted her weight and wished he'd get to the point. "So...what was it?"

"You ready for this? `Ding-dong the witch is dead.' Can you figure that one out?"

Molly could, but didn't bother enlightening him. She asked, "Do you have samples your customers have used in the past? Maybe it will give me an idea."

He reached behind to a lower shelf and pulled out a ledger. "Here, help yourself. My engraving orders from God knows when."

Molly eagerly began thumbing through the pages starting at the back. She spotted it immediately. "Verna on top side. Without Indiscretion. Bob on back. 9/22/95."

"Oh, this is a good one. And I know where it's from."

She turned the book around to show Nick, making up the story as she went along.

"It's from Shelley's sonnets...'Oh, the beauty of your love...uh...will be remembered always without indiscretion.'" Not bad, she thought, for a rush job.

He nodded appreciatively. "You're a smart one."

"Thank you," she murmured modestly, knowing Shelley would bolt upright in his coffin if he'd heard her crediting him for those invented lines.

Nick waited patiently while Molly appeared to be deciding on one of the bracelets. "That was an artsy-fartsy man that bought that bracelet," he said.

"Artsy-fartsy?"

"I remember him. He wasn't exactly one of my typical customers. Money, distinguished, you know, talked about these here paintings. From the French school, you know. Especially that one."

He pointed to a watercolor hanging on the wall. The delicate colors and impressionistic style were a marked contrast to the musty old oils in heavy baroque frames that cluttered his shop.

"What did he say about it?"

"Oh, that it was modeled after Manet's work. See, we buy out estates and..."

"What else did he say?"

"He knew his art pretty well. I could tell, the way he was looking at the pictures. He really liked this one. I thought for sure I had a sale. I don't ask any questions. By the way, lady, which one do you want?"

"Which what?"

"Bracelet. Which one do you want?"

"I can't make up my mind. I think maybe I should bring my daughter in and let her pick it out. It's for her."

"Good idea. That way you won't buy the wrong one." Nick replaced the bracelets in the window.

"Did that man buy a painting?" Molly called after him.

"No. He only liked the watercolor. Said he already had one at home." He laughed at his little joke. "So, some days, win a few...lose a few."

Molly felt obligated to buy something from Nick for his trouble. What she learned was certainly worth the cost of one bracelet. "I'll take that narrow one, the first one you showed me."

He looked at her wearily, and crawled back into the window. "That's what I said. Win a few, lose a few."

❧ TWELVE

"Thought you'd want to know, Stan, the lab got two sets of prints and a whole lot of smudges from the envelope. One set matches the girl's prints, from the right hand that was attached and the severed left one. The other set probably belongs to the sender. But that's your department."

Beltz grunted and was about to hang up when the lab technician added, "Wait a minute. There's a difference in the fingers. The nail beds of the left, the severed one, are scarred and deeply indented, typical beds of a nail biter."

"So?"

"The right one is normal."

"If you're a nail biter," Beltz asked, "wouldn't you bite the nails on both hands?"

"Yep."

After learning who lived at R.R.#5 from the Fort Wayne Police Department, Beltz dialed the number of the Carl Fitch house.

"Am I speaking to Carl Fitch?"

"Yes. Who is this?"

"This is Lieutenant Stanley Beltz, Area Three, Chicago Police Department."

"Police? What do you want?"

"We need some information about someone named Verna Lake. Do you know anyone by that name?"

"Verna Lake?" Carl repeated. "I sure don't know that name."

"You don't. Is there anyone else there I can speak with? Your wife perhaps?"

"Yeah. What was your name again?"

Beltz sighed. The same old civilian disbelief when it came to telephone calls. How do you flash a badge over the phone. "Lieutenant Stanley Beltz. You want to call me back here at the station?"

"No, no, that's okay. I'll get my wife."

The receiver, undoubtedly dropped from a wall phone, banged back and forth. Beltz heard Carl bellow for his wife.

"Hello. This is May Fitch," a timid voice answered.

"Mrs. Fitch, this is Lieutenant Beltz of the…"

"Yes, the Chicago police. Carl just told me. How can I help you?"

"Mrs. Fitch, do you know a Verna Lake?"

After a slight pause, May said, "No…I've never heard the name, Detective Beltz. Why are you calling us? How did you get our name?"

"We came across your address in our investigation."

"Of what?"

"Homicide."

"This…Verna Lake?"

"Yes."

"And you found our address? Where? You sure? Rural route number 5?"

"That's right. It was on an envelope among the dead girl's effects."

"That hardly seems possible. You must have read the address wrong."

"No ma'am, I have it right in front of me."

"An envelope, you say?"

"Yes ma'am."

"Who signed the letter?"

"We can't make out the signature." Beltz knew there was no letter, but sometimes a bluff paid off.

"Well, I don't think we can help you. My husband and I don't know...what was the name? Verna Lake? No, we don't know her. Besides, I haven't written any letters in the last two weeks."

Beltz thanked her and replaced the receiver. He reached for his suit jacket and grabbed his raincoat from the closet. He'd always wanted to see Fort Wayne in the fall.

Since a small boy, Stanley Beltz had been an avid reader, especially of the classics. He attributed his hobby to Miss Fogelson, his eighth grade English teacher. She had instilled in him a love for words, language, a well-turned phrase. Under her tutelage the class read Edison Marshall and O.Henry and Milton, and made shoe-box dioramas of the important scenes in each plot.

He devoured the required reading and with the local librarian's help, went further into classical literature. He never needed the Cliffs Notes; his recall was excellent, bringing back time and again most of what he read then and in his college years.

His pretty wife Lily had scolded him during their first married year. "If you aren't working a double shift on patrol or chasing bandits down a dark street, or whatever it is you do out there, you've got your nose stuck in a book."

He had laughed and picked her up, carrying his slender young wife easily to the sofa. "You married a cop, my dear, and everyone knows, 'A Policeman's Lot is not a Happy One!'"

He had sung this last, using all the Gilbert and Sullivan nonsense to make her laugh. She did, but the smile faded. "And what about your reading? Am I so boring you have to turn to books for excitement?"

"Ah, that," he said, "is to further my education. Your father wanted you to marry a rich man. How am I to rise in my profession, provide you with everything he wished you if..."

"Be serious, Stanley, enough with the books already." Her soft brown eyes had danced with mischief then, and she put her arms around him, saying softly, "Let's fool around."

Oh, how he had loved Lily. How do you start over at fifty-six to find another one.

As he drove to Indiana Saturday afternoon, the words engraved on the bracelet plagued him. He knew them. He had read them or heard them before. He had lain awake the last two nights for hours trying to figure out where, before finally falling asleep. It would come to him eventually. It always did. If there was ever a trivia contest of obscure phrases or quotations, Beltz would win hands down. Except for this one. Right now he'd lose the whole bundle.

The post box went by in a blur, and he slowed the car and turned around. He found the white clapboard house far back at the end of a gravel driveway, nestled in some scrubby woods.

He left the car and walked past the open garage with old farm machinery and lawn equipment rusting within. He thought about the Jonathan Winters routine, the rural scene, and the inevitable old barking dog with an infected ear. He was smiling at that when he rang the bell.

Several minutes passed, and while he waited, he had the eerie sensation of being watched from an upstairs window. He looked up and saw a curtain flutter closed.

A woman's face peered out at him through the porch window.

"Yes? What is it?"

"Detective Beltz, ma'am, from Chicago. Are you Mrs. Fitch?"

"Yes. Why did you come?" Her face was colorless, transparent as a piece of tracing paper, with tiny blue veins visible through the skin. He'd never seen a living person that pale before.

"If you don't mind, Mrs. Fitch, can I come inside and talk to you?"

While he spoke, Beltz had taken his shield and I.D. from his jacket pocket and held them to the window. "Just a few minutes, ma'am."

May opened the door and motioned for him to enter. The house smelled musty. There was a strong odor of urine. Shades had been pulled although the day was overcast, and it was dreary inside. Crocheted antimacassars stretched over the backs and arms of upholstered furniture, and small woven pads were placed under lamps and knick-knacks to guard against scratching the polished tables. A threadbare oriental rug lay in the center of the living-room floor, an ugly beige and blue Chinese, cheap when it was new.

A black cat sat atop a hutch, glaring balefully at Beltz. Another, an orange tabby, suddenly zipped through the room and disappeared.

Through the open door to the kitchen, Beltz could see a huge hulk of a man sitting at the window. His body seemed too big for the chair.

May called, "Carl, come in here. The Chicago policeman wants to talk to us, though I can't imagine why."

As she sat down on the edge of a needlepoint chair, Carl lumbered into the room, nodded to Beltz, and fell heavily onto the couch. Beltz remained standing.

"I had to come see you in person, Mr. and Mrs. Fitch, because in a murder investigation, we need to talk to anyone who might have known the victim."

"I told you I didn't know her...what's her name...and my husband didn't either."

"Is there anyone else living here?"

"Just us two."

A scruffy tomcat appeared suddenly and began rubbing against Beltz's leg. Absent mindedly, he petted it.

"No children?" he asked.

"No." May said the word at exactly the same time Carl said, "Yes, we have a son."

"Well," May said quickly, "he's not living here now."

"Oh? Where is he?"

"He lives in Chicago," Carl said, his small squinched eyes looking off in the distance. "Goes to art school there."

"He's quite a good artist," May cut in, "even won a scholarship. That picture there, above the fireplace, won first prize in the Fort Wayne Junior Chamber of Commerce contest. When he was in high school."

Beltz looked at the watercolor still life, a copper bowl holding three juicy oranges and a ripe banana. The fruit looked real.

"That's very good," he said. "Are the rest of these paintings his work, too?"

The walls were hung with still lifes and landscapes, and caricatures in charcoal, and as Beltz walked closer, he could make out the artist's signature: Verne F. Hair stood up on the back of his neck.

"Have you any pictures of your son?"

Carl rose and walked to a desk in the corner. "Here's one, taken at his high school graduation."

Beltz took the framed picture from Carl and looked at it closely. In color, it showed a young handsome blond boy standing in cap and gown between his proud parents. The picture was grainy, enlarged, most likely, from a 110 negative.

But it was easy to see the boy was small, barely taller than his mother and completely dwarfed by Carl. Beltz knew the face. It was the same face.

"I see your son's name is Verne, right?"

"Yes, Verne," May said.

Beltz put the picture back on the desk. "When did you see him last?"

Carl spoke up. "He was home at Christmas." He glanced at his wife, expecting her to continue.

But Beltz saw an opportunity and framed his next question carefully. "How did he look to you?"

"Same as always," May said, "too thin. Never eats enough."

"Does he like living in Chicago, or is he lonely in the big city?" Beltz looked sympathetic. "A far cry from Fort Wayne."

"Oh, he likes it all right. Even sold some of his paintings."

"Do you know where your son lives?"

"Well, he does move around a lot," May said. "Every time they raise the rent on him, he has to look for another room. He lives with a Mrs. Minkoff. It's a nice house. He doesn't have much money, you know."

Carl nodded.

Beltz knew the real reason for the P.O. Box now, but he wasn't ready to tell them, not yet. "Do you have another picture of Verne? A recent snapshot, maybe?"

May opened a large scrapbook on an end table and turned a few pages. "This one here was taken last Christmas when he was home."

Beltz looked over her shoulder at the print.

He sighed deeply. "I have something important to tell you."

❧ THIRTEEN

The two-hour drive back to Chicago had not eased Lieutenant Stanley Beltz's mind; he was still distressed. Telling the Fitches their son was dead had been ordeal enough. It hardly seemed kind or even necessary at the time to inform them of his sex change. After all, they would only be shown the face at the morgue for identification. But as he sorted out and explained the essential details of the murder to them, he realized he should not be the one to break this news. A pastor, perhaps, or a friend.

He was still puzzled at their reaction to Verne's death. They had sat like lumps, listening to his words, May's head shaking back and forth as though he was making a terrible mistake, Carl's face turning a pasty, deathly white. But not a sob, not a tear.

As he rolled along the state highway bordered by small farms, he realized why they had been so eager for him to leave. To the outside world, the Fitches were as cold and rigid as the icicles on a barn roof in the dead of winter. But when alone, surely the hard exterior would melt quickly into a flood of sorrow. That's when they didn't want him around.

He followed the signs on the Calumet Expressway, angled his '87 Pontiac into the Dan Ryan, and watched the farm land

and rural houses disappear, replaced by the stark hi-rises of the south side housing projects. He passed Comiskey Park and the yawning spaces between burned-out buildings, and his policeman's soul was full of pain for all the little children who played in the debris.

Dispatch called him on the radio.

"Beltz here."

"Lieutenant, a Mrs. Pearl Minkoff wants you to stop by and see her. Something to do with the Lake homicide."

"I'm so glad you're here. I found something absolutely dreadful and I don't know what to do. I can't imagine anyone having this in their room. I mean, when I saw it, I got sick to my stomach. I..."

"All right, Mrs. Minkoff, you just calm down now and tell me what this is all about."

Pearl brought Stanley Beltz into the front room and motioned for him to sit. "I spent the last few hours getting Verna's things together. All of her personal possessions that should go to her next of kin, when you find them. You know I can't afford to keep the apartment empty too long."

Her words tumbled out, and as she spoke, she wiped her hands nervously on the front of her apron. Her face was flushed and perspiring.

"It's...it's in her room. I just left it. You'll have to go up and see for yourself."

"All right, let's go upstairs. You lead the way," Beltz said, taking her arm.

She kept up a running commentary as they climbed the stairs. "It all happened when I started to pack her wigs in a box. Five of them. Blonde, red, black...you know, short, pageboy, one with bangs, one curly like a perm...I just took them off the stands to put them all together in a big box I was packing. Her clothes, her shoes, twenty pairs...can you imagine? Who can wear all those shoes? She was very vain, I guess...then there was a radio and a record player, and all those cosmetics. It took me a long time."

They stopped at the top of the stairs and Pearl leaned against the railing, out of breath. "Then I went to her dresser, and all the time I'm checking the list the officers left...you know, the inventory sheet? And there was this doll...a small cloth doll, like the kind you win at the amusement park...for knocking over all the pins? It was stuck in the back of the drawer, all crinkled, so I pulled it out. And that...that thing fell off. It was tacked on to the dolly's head."

She shuddered involuntarily. "Lieutenant Beltz, look at it! There it is," she cried, pointing into the room, "right on the floor where it dropped. What does it look like to you?"

Beltz walked in, kneeled down, and picked up the object. He turned it over in his hand. The center was stiff and curled, like an old dried-up grapefruit rind. The top was covered with coarse black hair.

"What is that thing, My God! what is it?" Pearl cried from the doorway.

"I think you know what it is, Mrs. Minkoff, that's why you're so upset," Beltz said quietly. "It's obviously a scalp."

She closed her eyes tightly and grimaced in disgust. "You mean...a person's scalp?"

Beltz stood. "We'll have to check it out."

"But what would she be doing with a scalp? And on a dolly's head. What kind of a business is that? And where did she get it?"

Beltz looked at her for a moment. "Maybe from an Indian, Mrs. Minkoff."

"Why did you lie, Chief?"

"I was afraid."

"Afraid of what?"

"You said she was missing. I was afraid you'd pin something on me."

"When I talked to you, Chief, she was just a missing person. So what could I pin on you?"

"Oh, you know. Cops."

Beltz also knew more about George Burning Tree, that he was a good athlete and kept to himself. That he was known in Uptown for the American flag he sported on each bulging bicep of his long arms, and the winning basketball team he coached at the Indian Center. In warm weather, hefting heavy furniture in undershirt and jeans for the Apollo Moving Company, each flag seemed to wave in the breeze, causing little girls to laugh and grown-up ladies to sigh.

Beltz also knew something the moving company had told him when George first came to work. The Indian had not uttered a word. Initially, they thought him a deaf mute, but one day a chair dropped on George's foot and he yelled, "SHIT!" and they realized he could speak and just never bothered to.

Now Lieutenant Beltz and George Burning Tree sat across a desk from each other in the interrogation room at Area Three Headquarters. The Indian had been brought in for questioning an hour ago. It had been very slow going. It was hard enough to get more than a few words at a time from him. Now that he was a suspect in a homicide, he was even more tight-lipped.

"How long had you been seeing her?"

"Not long."

"How long?"

"Three — four weeks."

"For sex?"

George thought for a minute. "It started out that way."

"How did it change?"

"I don't know. Maybe I loved her."

"*Maybe* you loved her?"

"I'm not sure. Maybe."

Beltz poured coffee into two mugs and slid one across the desk. "Black, right? Listen, Chief, we've known each other a long time. You've always been honest with me."

"I am now."

Beltz sat forward and peered at George intently. "When was the last time you saw Verna?"

"A week ago, Thursday."

"She seem okay then?"

George sat slumped in his chair, his hands clasped between his legs. His long black hair fell forward, concealing his face.

"Lieutenant," he said, his voice thick and low, "I didn't hurt Verna. That girl was precious to me. Like a doll. So delicate, and white, and small."

"A doll, huh?" Beltz opened the bottom drawer of his desk and withdrew a small evidence bag. He placed it on the desk and opened it, removing the cloth doll and scalp. "You ever see this before?"

"Yes."

"Where?"

"Shit, Beltz, you know where."

"I'm asking you where, Chief."

"On Verna's dresser."

"You give it to her?"

"Not the doll."

"The scalp?"

George nodded.

"Where did you get it?"

"From my father."

"Where did he get it?"

"From his father."

"What tribe were your people?"

"Sioux."

"Where?"

"South Dakota."

"You grow up there?"

"Yeah."

"They keep lots of scalps?"

"Only the prize ones."

Beltz wondered what it would take to provoke a reaction from this great stone face. "You ever scalp anyone?"

"No."

"What's a prize scalp, then?"

George met Beltz's eyes for the first time since the interrogation began. He let a few seconds pass, then said,

"I'll tell you a story. War was a game... long before I was born. My grandfather was a brave warrior. He counted many coups. That means brave deeds. One day, women and children were alone in the camp when four white men rode in. They stole food and guns...and did cruel things. Some children died. The camp was burned. My grandmother was raped and killed, her body cut apart."

George picked up the scalp. "Grandfather searched for the killer. It took one year. When he found him, he cut him up in many pieces and took his scalp for a prize."

Beltz frowned. "An eye for an eye, eh? If it was such a Goddam prize, how could you give it away?"

"I promised Verna a present."

"But you didn't give her the doll."

"No. She had it."

"Where'd she get it?"

"I don't know."

"You and Verna ever have a fight?"

"It wasn't a fight."

"*What* wasn't a fight?"

"When I told her the story about the scalp. She laughed. She said, 'You count coups with me?' Then she touched her long yellow hair. She laughed and laughed. She said, 'Is my hair safe?'"

"This made you mad?"

"Yes."

"What did you do?"

"I hit her."

"Where?"

"Across her laughing face."

"This the only time you hit her?"

"Other times are not important."

"Got a bad temper, huh Chief?"

The room was silent. Neither man moved. George's eyes were flat and cold, and he spat out his next words.

"I didn't kill her."

George knew he had a bad temper. He knew, too, that sometimes he scared people. Not because he was a big man; big men could be jolly, funny, good-humored. It was not that he was devoid of humor, although his mien was dour. And it was not the few words he used, it was the fact that he used so few. His taciturnity was unsettling, and he had been this way since that terrible afternoon of his twelfth birthday when grief and anger had branded his dying brother's words in his mind.

Words had been a big part of George's youth. Growing up on the reservation was a lengthy course in wise sayings; the elders had a million of them.

As a little boy, George would squat outside their meeting hall for hours, squirreling away enough words for two lifetimes. Not all of them made sense. When he needed explanations, he would run to his older brother, Black Eagle, who always seemed to know the answers. When he didn't, he made them up, a fact George did not wise up to until much later.

"Must I always live here?" he had asked his brother one day.

"No. When you grow up you can leave. I will when I'm twenty-one."

"Where will you go?"

Black Eagle straightened his shoulders and stood as he had seen the elders pose in the meeting hall. "I am going to college, little one, where I can learn to be a doctor. And then I will come back and take care of the sick people here."

"Can I do that too?"

"Yes. But you must always remember your people come first. The white man can plant the seed but we must harvest the crop."

George was eight years old then, and idolized his teenaged brother, following him around, playing ball and fishing and sledding down the big hills in winter. Four years later Black Eagle died, his big brown body consumed in three days by meningitis.

During this time George never left his brother's side, soothing him with cool rags and a stream of comforting words.

"You'll be better soon...I know you will. When I was at the edge of the forest I saw the eggs of the blue bird...that's a good sign. And I had a dream...we were fishing together and you caught the biggest fish I had ever seen. And the elders met today and they say..."

"Hush." Black Eagle's voice was hoarse and thready. He strained to get the words out. With a sudden surge of strength he gripped George's shirt, pulling him close.

"Remember this. Words fly like raindrops against the leaves. It is better to listen with two ears than speak with one tongue."

Numb with grief, anger eventually taking the place of tears, George forgot any thought of the idealized life he and Black Eagle had planned. As the years passed, with no encouragement from his parents who continued to grieve for their first-born son, George's only thought was to get out.

The day after high school graduation, he boarded the first bus leaving Rosebud, South Dakota. The destination sign read CHICAGO. It made no difference to George.

In the fifteen years he had lived in Uptown, he often wondered if his brother's spirit was at peace. Perhaps working with their people at the Center could make it so. Now George listened with two ears, and rarely spoke with one tongue.

———

"Sorry to bother you on a Saturday night, Mr. Persakis," Beltz said into the phone, "but this is a homicide investigation."

"Aw, for Christ's sake, I've got a house full of people here. We're watching the wrestling matches."

"It'll just take a minute, Mr. Persakis."

"Who was killed?"

"One of our cases, Sir."

"Who did you say you were again?"

"Lieutenant Stanley Beltz, Area Three, shield number..."

"Awright, awright, what do you want to know? Just make it quick."

"Does George Burning Tree work for you?"

"Yeah, why? Was it him? Is he in trouble?"

"No, just checking. How long has he been in your employ?"

"Oh...let's see, maybe two years."

"Did he have references?"

"I think so. My file's in the office. But I usually hire nobody without he has some references."

"Is he a good worker?"

"Yeah. No complaints. He does his job. He don't talk too much, though. But that's all right with me. If they get into gab-fests, it only costs me money."

"Is he dependable?"

"Yeah. That's the funny part. He don't drink. Them Indians drink, you know. But George, he's always on the job."

"No problems at all?"

"Yeah, well, he's got a lousy temper. Got into two fights with some of the men. Broke a nose, knocked some teeth out, and I told him one more time and he's out on his ass."

"When was this?"

"Last few months. Is that all you want to know...cause I got a house full of people here..."

"That's all, Mr. Persakis. I appreciate your taking the time. You go back to your wrestling."

❧ FOURTEEN

Molly Fast settled herself cross-legged on the bedroom window seat, phone in hand, to find Verna's elusive and erudite lover.

Pearl Minkoff had given her a sketchy description: a well-dressed man in his forties, young looking, with a full head of gray hair and a gray mustache. He had a perpetual sun tan and always visited on Mondays, perhaps Thursdays, too. It wasn't much to go on. And what had she learned from Nick, the jeweler? That he had sold a bracelet with a strange inscription and the male customer had an obvious interest in art.

His first name could be Bob — Robert what? It might be a nickname. Or acronym. There must be two million sun-tanned gray haired well-dressed Bobs running around town.

Molly held the Chicago phone book in her lap, and starting with the A's, began calling the art galleries in town.

Since becoming a widower, Stanley Beltz didn't mind working on Sundays. Occasionally he traded shifts with the other men when Lily was alive. They had usually spent their Sundays at the Art Institute or the Field Museum. Lily was certain she was Nefertiti in a former life and lingered in the Egyptian rooms "soaking up her heritage." Stanley would humor her. It gave him a chance to gawk at the huge stuffed elephants in the great hall. As a child, he had been fascinated by their leathery wrinkled hides, touching them surreptitiously until a guard would gently shoo him away. He could never admit to Lily that they still fascinated him.

They rarely missed the opening of a new gallery, even though for many years they couldn't afford to buy paintings on a patrolman's salary. When he made detective, their first splurge was a 16 x 20 oil they had long admired, and it hung over the living-room mantle until after Lily's death.

He rarely used that room anymore, spending most of his time in the kitchen and den. The only change he made in the house was to move the painting to the wall at the foot of his bed. The brightly colored circus was the first and last thing he saw every day.

Now there was no reason to be home on Sunday. In a quiet office he was able to complete a lot of paper work. His typing was slow and he dreaded filling out police reports. If he had been more diligent in typing class, instead of sneaking Dickens between the covers of his basic Gregg, this work might be less tedious.

It was like that today. This bitch of a homicide: the victim was a woman who was once a man, the parents were obviously lying and seemingly unbereaved, and he wasn't sure about his one good suspect either.

This morning he'd only had coffee, and that must have been brewed by one of the hung-over detectives. Now at noon, he was hungry and tired, and when Molly Fast walked into the office, the red rose bobbing on her lapel, she was the last person in the world he wanted to see.

The contrast between them was striking. Though close in age, Molly looked fresh and energetic, Beltz looked washed-out and stooped. He nevertheless put on a broad smile when she sat down.

"Mrs. Fast, how's your book going?"

Molly grinned. "If things don't get better, depend on it, they'll get worse."

"Oh," he said, surprised, but tapping his foot under the desk, impatient.

"I've been doing some leg work. Don't worry, nothing illegal or immoral."

Beltz leaned forward on the desk and gazed directly at Molly. "Mrs. Fast, exactly what are you talking about?"

"The murder. Verna Lake's murder."

"Why does this case interest you?"

"I suppose I'd better start at the beginning."

"I'm listening."

She paused, bit her lower lip, sighed deeply, and said, "Lieutenant Beltz, did you ever wonder how that hand got into the squad car?"

"Oh, c'mon, don't tell me you know?"

"Sure. It was me. I put it there."

"When? Why?" he asked sharply.

"Wait a minute. Let me tell you how it all started, in my own way. I was working on this book. So I dressed as a bag lady, found the hand in a garbage can and then I had to get it to the police so I dropped it in the squad car when the cops ran into the hospital."

She hesitated. "Why are you looking at me like that?"

"Go on, Mrs. Fast, there must be more."

Molly then related how she learned about Verna, her conversation with Pearl, and her subsequent follow-up of the bracelet. "I realize you're investigating the same thing, but I had this crazy hunch."

"Tell me."

"Well, I tracked him down."

"Who?"

"Bob. Remember? Without indiscretion—Bob? On the bracelet."

"How did you know about the bracelet?"

"Mrs. Minkoff told me."

"A veritable fount of information," Beltz said dryly. "What do you mean—track him down.?"

"I found him. It wasn't simple. I spent hours on the phone, then running around to galleries looking for a Bob with gray hair and a mustache — a snappy dresser with a suntan, yet."

"You mean you found the man who gave her the bracelet? Mrs. Fast, I have three detectives working on this, so far checking out thirty-seven jewelry stores in Chicago." He waved a report in his hand. "Thirty seven jewelry stores, Mrs. Fast, and you think you've found him."

"I'm sure they're doing a good job," she said, "but I told you I had this crazy hunch. I only went to seven stores in Uptown. And maybe I was lucky. I hit it on the seventh and I think I found the right man. You be the judge. And of course, you take it from here."

"Well, thank you. Would you like to share this information with me?"

Molly read through her notes. "His name is Robert Markham. He and his wife own the Markham Galleries on Lake Shore Drive."

Beltz interrupted. "And he fits the description, right? Tell me, how come the tie-in with the art galleries?"

Molly told Beltz about Nick's Uptown Jewelers on Clark Street, and how the shop was filled with odds and ends the owner had acquired from estate sales. Nick had told her of the man who bought the bracelet commenting about some of the paintings for sale. How he seemed so knowledgeable, especially about one painting that caught his eye.

"I just put two and two together."

Beltz shook his head in disbelief. "Maybe we should put you on the payroll, Mrs. Fast."

"You can call me Molly." She was not wearing her glasses and her eyes were enormous, the brightest blue Beltz had ever seen. In spite of his initial annoyance, he was beginning to feel glad she was there. And it wasn't just because of the new information, which was valuable, he had to admit.

He leaned back and studied her for a long time.

Molly sat patiently, waiting for him to say something.

Finally he rose, feeling not quite as tired, walked around the desk and perched on the edge.

"I have to tell you this has been a surprise, and I intend to follow it up." He grimaced with a hand on his stomach. "You know, this morning's coffee is burning a hole in my gut, and I've got to have lunch. I want to talk about this some more. Will you join me?"

"Does that mean you're not angry?"

"No. It just means I'm starved."

ઝ FIFTEEN

Verne Fitch made the most important decision of his life the same day he sold the paintings to Ellie Markham. Maybe it was the early spring, with the sweet fragrance of crab-apple blossoms blooming in a pink and white cloud along the lake-front. Or perhaps it was the new growth all around him, pushing its way through cracks in the sidewalks or popping open overnight on the bare trees, turning them into a splash of green lace against the blue sky. Whatever triggered his decision, Verne knew that he wanted, more than anything in the world, to feel like that: new born and fresh.

Doctor Hersey had been urging him to put his dreams down on paper, to use his talent in a way unavailable to most of his patients.

"Draw your dreams, my boy, lay them out on canvas with broad strokes of bold color and then look at them, know them, own them. And then, be free of them."

The doctor had been saying that for months, but Verne had refused to listen, afraid that by doing as the doctor suggested, he would be fouling his work with the hideously erotic and repeated nightmares he'd endured since childhood.

They struck a compromise: Verne would continue to paint his conscious dreams and fancies and work with the doctor in

91

their weekly sessions. But the nightmares were too grotesque, too revealing. They were not for anyone to see.

He had delivered the paintings to Ellie at her Lake Shore Drive gallery, signed the contract giving the Markhams exclusive use of his talents, then headed for his appointment with Dr. Hersey.

To Verne, the doctor looked like a bird, his small body slightly hunched, feet splayed and not quite touching the floor when he sat, his shock of red hair sticking straight up like a crested cardinal.

He sat now, watching Verne, pad and pencil in his lap.

"So why today, Verne? What makes this day different from all other days?"

Verne had missed the religious word-play, but smiled and said, "I suppose it's the spring. Everything's bursting into bloom, a renewal of life all around me, it seems the right time to grab for the chance to be reborn. It's right. I feel it's the right time. Don't you agree?"

"Verne, it's not up to me to agree or disagree with you. This is a very serious decision, and only you can say yes or no to it. The medical community can do their best to advise you, to evaluate your motives and to look on you as a candidate for this kind of surgery. You've had the hormone therapy, you've seen other doctors, we've gone over and over the same ground for months. If you feel continuing your life as a man is too great an abomination..."

"I've always felt that way," Verne cried, up now and pacing the floor. "I've never been at peace. Ever since I can remember, I've hated what I am. I've always felt like a woman inside, screaming to get out, to be recognized. I've had to repress all of my desires, my tastes, my needs, to conform to the way the rest of the world sees me. I can't do it any more. Dr. Hersey, I've got to have that operation."

The doctor laid aside his pad and leaned forward, elbows resting on his knees. Even in his agitated state, Verne saw him as the cardinal about to settle into the bird-bath.

"You must, my dear friend, bear in mind that this operation will not solve all your problems. In fact, it might very well pose some new ones, the kind you cannot even anticipate at this time."

"You've helped me with most of my problems, you must know that, Dr. Hersey. And the new ones you speak of...well, I can cope with them. Once I'm in a body I feel comfortable with, I think I can take care of the rest."

The doctor shifted on his chair and frowned, the look in his eyes belying the cool, impersonal tone of voice.

"I must tell you, Verne, the pain will be unbearable for a time. And we've talked about the social repercussions. Most people will not understand or care about your psyche. Some friends will drift away. You'll be that freak who changed his sex."

This was tough cruel talk, but Verne knew what Dr. Hersey was up to. Lay it on thick and don't leave out a thing so that every base is covered. There is no turning back.

Later, walking home through the park, he thought about this conversation and realized how lucky he had been to find this compassionate and wise man. He loved him, really. Verne had never loved a man like that before, as a son loves a father.

Coming up on a slight rise, he glimpsed an older man with a small child, probably a grandchild, holding a balloon high above his head. The little boy laughed and squealed with delight as the old man tugged on the string, making it dance in the warm afternoon air.

Verne watched and shuddered. The happy sight was a bitter contrast to the sudden memories, of a grandfather who stroked his arm in a darkened shed, who kissed him on the mouth, tasting of tobacco juice and raw onion, who took the small boy's hand and made him rub the old man's stained and dampened crotch. And all the while, the emerald eyes of the gold snake glittered as they caught the light coming through the small window. He was sickened now, and turned his eyes away.

Paint a picture, Dr. Hersey had said, lay it out, look at it, and be free of it once and for all. No chance, Doc. No painting of that wet-lipped, masturbating old hypocrite, who preached of Satan and eternal hell-fire if you strayed from the path of righteousness, would ever free Little Verne of those ugly afternoons.

To rid himself of the bad taste, Verne stopped to buy a gelato cone from a street vendor. With the first lick of his tongue around the edge of the blueberry cream, he was aware of how good it tasted, that it had never tasted this good before.

The dark thoughts sailed away with the little boy's balloon, and the sun shone brighter, the birds sang sweeter, and Verne walked with new vigor in his step. He could think of no reason in the world why it shouldn't always be this way.

❧ SIXTEEN

"This place has wicked apple pancakes, loaded with cinnamon." Beltz grinned. "And cholesterol."

They sat at a table by the window of the Lockup, a favored hangout for the Belmont Area's local constabulary. The sun's glare played havoc with the hand lettered menu, and because Molly was still uncomfortable with new contacts, she went along with the pancakes.

He gave their order to the waitress and went right to the subject.

"First off, Molly, you've been clever enough to beat our men to the punch, and you've given us a valuable bit of information."

"You are too kind," Molly said, smiling.

"But I can't emphasize this too strongly...you've got to stop. Number one, it's too dangerous. Number two, you are not an authorized officer of the police department and that opens up a hornet's nest of problems, like law suits and jeopardizing of evidence. Judges have thrown out cases for a helluva lot less."

Molly's smile faded. "Why are you making such a *tsimmes* out of this. Are you angry?"

Beltz looked at her, surprised, but said only, "Not exactly angry. I want to protect you and the case."

"But I found a likely suspect."

"That's police business," he said harshly. "I can understand how you feel, finding the hand and all, and if you want to play Miss Marple, God knows another opinion could be useful."

Molly bristled at the odious comparison to Christie's elderly spinster detective. Drumming her fingers on the table, she croaked, "It should be cozy sitting by the fire, tatting a nice afghan for these old bones." She flushed, then spoke brightly. "All right, if that's the role I'm assigned to play."

"Good. And my friends call me Stan or Stanley, sometimes Stash."

Molly ignored his attempt to placate her. "I hope you're going to check out this Bob Markham."

"Of course."

"I have the feeling that if you thought he was such a hot prospect, we wouldn't be here having lunch."

"Tell me more about Markham."

"Robert Markham, married to Ellie Markham. Their art gallery is in their apartment on Lake Shore Drive." She added smugly, "I told them I was the designer for American Hospital Supply's new offices. That's how I got in. Anyway, they deal mostly in modern art, selling to business firms and corporate offices. From what I could see, they show a lot of watercolors, you know, seascapes, shimmering lakes, painted deserts, that sort of thing, the stuff decorators like to match to sofas…and some pastel portraits and a few charcoal cartoons, clever as…"

Beltz put down a forkful of pancake. "Repeat that."

"What?"

"The last part."

"Pastel portraits? Charcoal…"

"Yeah, charcoal." He drained his coffee cup. "Tell me again about this Nick's Jewelers."

"Well, the funny thing about that inscription on the bracelet was after I found it in his order book, everything else fell into place."

"Ah yes, that elusive inscription."

"Without Indiscretion — Bob," Molly said aloud, trying to jog her own memory. She laughed. "I even pretended I knew where it was from. I made up a whole spiel. Said it was from Shelley's sonnets. He believed me, too."

Beltz looked at her a moment, then suddenly stood, grabbed her by the arm, and walked quickly with her to the door.

"Come with me."

Hurrying to keep up with him, Molly cast a longing glance at half of the delicious pancake left untouched on her plate.

With Molly waiting in his car listening to a tape of Benny Goodman and the Chicago Symphony, Beltz rode the elevator up to the Markham apartment. The paneling was distinctive; the builder had tastefully chosen walnut for the elevator, not the plastic imitation. The door opened on the twenty-second floor. 22A was directly to the left. Unlike most buildings in town where the search for the right apartment was as long as the hallway, this building had class. Only A and B on each floor.

He tapped the door knocker and heard the first four measures of Beethoven's Fifth echo inside the apartment.

"Yes?" a woman's voice called; he knew he was being appraised through the peephole.

"Lieutenant Stanley Beltz, Belmont Area, Mrs. Markham. May I have a moment of your time?"

A latch was pulled back and the door opened. "How can I help you? Lieutenant Beltz, did you say?"

He flashed his shield.

"Come in, please."

He followed her into the all white living room, the intense

blue of the lake beyond the wall of windows the only accent of color.

In her plain gray cotton dress reaching to her ankles and her colorless face, the woman did nothing to perk up the mono-chromatic color scheme.

"What is this about?" she asked.

"You are Mrs. Markham?"

"Yes."

"Is your husband home?"

"No."

"Your husband is Robert Markham, correct?"

"Yes."

"And you and your husband have a gallery on the premises?"

"Well, yes, but why are you asking me that?" She ran a hand nervously through her light brown hair, unfashionably cut in what Beltz would describe as a Buster Brown style. "You know, we've been here for years. The building okayed our use of some of our rooms for displaying the work of our artists."

"That's not why I'm here. I have a few questions."

"About what?"

"Do you know a Verna Lake?"

She shook her head. "No, I don't."

"Do you recall ever meeting a woman by that name at one of your showings or at another gallery?"

Again she shook her head. "No. The name means nothing to me."

"Has Mr. Markham ever mentioned that name to you?"

"No. It's possible he knows her, but," she added cooley, "we're not together all the time."

An ornate clock chimed three-fifteen, and Beltz looked up. He recognized it as a Viennese Richter, similar to the one his mother prized so highly. It had chimed every fifteen minute period of his life until he left home. But this clock was bigger, had three heavy brass weights instead of two, and a magnificent swinging pendulum.

But his gaze lingered on a framed charcoal drawing of a little boy, a slingshot hanging out of his pocket, holding a broken bird in his hands. It hung next to the clock in an artful display of pictures, clock, and an old Spode platter.

"I must tell you," Beltz said, "this is a beautiful room. And the view is spectacular." He walked to the windows. "Spectacular."

"Lieutenant…"

"And your furnishings, your antiques are so interesting. I've always wanted an apartment like this."

He was looking at the lake and couldn't see Ellie's expression, the corner of her mouth twisting as she wondered how this rumpled, unstylish man would fit in her meticulous and studied home.

"Thank you," she said.

"And these paintings. I wish I could afford even one. Say, like that one. The drawing of the little boy. I can just feel his sadness."

"That is a lovely piece, isn't it?" Ellie said, off her guard. "It's one of my favorites. But it's not for sale."

"Any others like that? By the same artist?" He peered at the signature. "Verne F…what is the last name?"

"Fitch. His name is Verne Fitch. He's a very gifted young man. We have more of his work in the gallery, but they're not in charcoal. They're watercolors. He doesn't work in charcoal any more. Strictly watercolors now. But they're lovely. Would you like to see them?"

"That would be very nice of you."

Ellie led him through a hall door to a large room at the back of the apartment. It was wall to wall and floor to ceiling paintings. Colors jumped out at Beltz; blues and greens, scarlets and purples, bright orange and shadings of grays. It was a feast for the eye and he stood, captivated, taking it all in.

"Over here," Ellie said. "We only have three left. But we expect more soon."

"Terrific. So vibrant. That American flag waves in the breeze. Isn't this the Labor Day parade on State Street? A couple of months ago?"

"How clever of you. That's exactly what it is."

"I have to admit," Beltz said modestly, "I recognized the mayor's face. So this Fitch fellow gives you paintings right along?"

"Oh yes. Every few months. He's very dependable."

"When he brings them in, do you accept them automatically? That must be tricky. I mean, what if you don't like them? Do you tell him that?"

Ellie laughed. "When you sign an exclusive with an artist, you have already determined that he has talent, and it's most unlikely that you'd have to refuse his work. We accept everything. But not everything sells. Besides, he doesn't bring them in personally, he sends them by special messenger. That saves any embarrassment. But we've never had that problem."

"So," Beltz said innocently, "you haven't seen this young man, this Verne Fitch, since you signed him."

"That's right. We haven't seen him in over a year."

"Doesn't that seem strange?"

"Not really. We have several artists, some out of town, who send their work, and we send the checks. The ones who live in the city, well, maybe they can't cope with a part of themselves being given away. I can understand that. It's their creation."

Beltz, his hands stuffed in his pockets, moved around the gallery. "You and your husband always agree on the artists? Could be trouble, I guess, if you didn't." He chuckled.

Ellie stayed close to his heels; Beltz could smell her soaps-cented cologne. "We've had our little brou-ha-has. But our success in the business attests to the fact that we're usually right."

"He likes this Verne Fitch as much as I do?"

"Yes. Although he's never met him. I'm the one who discovered Verne. But we had no problem agreeing on that one. And Verne has never disappointed us."

"I'd sure like to live with that charcoal drawing for a while."

"I'm afraid I can't do that," she said quickly.

"Well, you've been very kind. When do you think it would be a good time to catch your husband at home?"

"He'll be here tomorrow afternoon. Call first, to make sure."

As the door closed, Ellie wandered back into the living room, suddenly aware that the detective never did explain the reason for his visit.

"Well, what do you think?" Molly asked eagerly, as Beltz started the engine. "Did I call it right?"

He shook his head. "You're a *nudzh*, you know that?"

"I'm a pest?"

"With this case you are. I'm the detective, remember? You're the writer cum designer cum whatever else you dream up in the next ten minutes!"

"This designer led you to the gallery," she said huffily. "And incidentally, why did we have to rush over here, *mitt'n derinnen?* I left my pancake. You owe me."

Beltz braked at a red light. "What's with these Yiddish idioms you keep using?"

"Colorful, right? I mean, there are certain words that say it all."

"Yeah, *I* know, but where did *you* learn them?"

She told him about her husband's nanny, a young Jewish girl who escaped from Germany before the war. His family sponsored her, and she had stayed on with them. Sky used to pepper his language with the Yiddish expressions he learned from her, and soon after they were married, Molly started using them too. "It's not so much the words as the sound. I mean, what else could *schlemiel* mean but stupid!"

Beltz laughed. "I have to agree with you."

Traffic was sparse. At times like this, he always wondered

why the computers couldn't speed up the interval between red and green on slow days.

"We rushed over here," he explained, "because, whether you know it or not, I suddenly remembered the Thomas Hardy novel I had to read in high school...that inscription, 'a lover without indiscretion is no lover at all,' is a line from it."

"So?"

He looked at her. "It's from The Hand of Ethelberta." He said it slowly, enunciating each word.

Horns honked impatiently behind him; he put the car in gear and drove on.

"Christ!" Molly whispered, touching Beltz's arm instinctively. "The hand. The bracelet. Bob. It all fits, doesn't it?"

"Ah, Molly, don't be wearing the fur coat while the bear is still dancing in the forest. A case isn't a case without evidence. And a suspect is just a suspect. Besides, lady," he added, touching her hand still resting on his arm, "you are off this case."

She drew away her hand slowly. "You really mean that? After all I've done for you?"

He smiled. "Ah, but what have you done for me lately?"

"What did you have in mind?"

"Don't you have to get home to hubby and the kids?"

"No hubby. He died last year." She gazed at the darkening sky, and said softly. "I don't have any children."

Beltz turned into Belmont Avenue and headed west. "I'm sorry. My wife died last year, too."

They fell silent. Street lights had come on and a brisk chill wind was picking up. Molly closed her window, thinking how cozy it was in the car with him. "You know," Beltz said, "since our lunch was cut short, why don't you have dinner with me. I hate eating alone."

"On one condition," Molly said, facing him. "Tell me what you think of Bob Markham. Is he a suspect or not?"

"He wasn't there."

"Then what were you doing up there all that time?"

"Looking at paintings. That's what you go to a gallery for, isn't it?"

"Lieutenant Beltz, you are infuriating! Can't you give a straight answer?"

Beltz grinned. "No. That's how you find things out."

While Molly freshened up in the Area Three bathroom, Beltz picked up messages and signed himself out.

"Hey, Lieutenant, you hear about the Chief?" the desk sergeant called out. "He was arrested a couple of hours ago."

"What the hell for?"

"Attempted murder!"

❧ SEVENTEEN

Casimir Putch suffered from chronic acne. At twenty-nine, his face sported the pits and pustules that accompanied this wretched affliction. Ignorance of deodorants and an unbathed appearance made him an unattractive addition to the clutch of regular crime reporters who hung around the Area Three station.

Caz was considered a drip, a whiner, a leech. He cadged scraps of information, hoping against hope that one of them would lead him to his big story. One time, just one time, he wanted an exclusive for the Daily Herald. His newspaper was a small neighborhood daily with a remarkably large and loyal readership. But nobody paid any attention to him.

Caz was on the lowest rung of the ladder, as far as the cops and his editor were concerned. When a big story broke, he was the last reporter to be assigned. Sometimes he would look in the mirror and wonder if he was invisible.

He didn't see the large ears sticking out from his narrow head like bat wings. He didn't see the sores or the thick lenses distorting his myopic eyes. He was not a pretty sight. And so tall and skinny that Beltz had dubbed him the noodle. The recruits didn't even know his name.

"Hey, Noodle," one of the detectives would call, looking up from his typewriter, "you're bothering me. Go over to the

Twenty-fourth...maybe there's a gang war going on."

"Noodle, do a public servant a big favor. I need a pick-me-up...a large coke with plenty of ice."

It was Noodle this...Noodle that. Mostly, they just ignored him.

The night they brought in the hand, Caz got wind of a big story. He'd been hanging around the station as usual, eavesdropping and peering over shoulders. The cops were joking around, betting on the sexy dimensions of the handless body. Caz kept quiet and listened, and the more he heard, the more determined he was to make this his big scoop. All he needed was one small break to lord it over those egomaniacs from the big papers.

In spite of doors slammed in his face, Caz pursued his questioning of Verna's neighbors and was finally convinced the hand belonged to the missing girl.

By this time, unfortunately for Caz, the body had been brought to the morgue and examined by the M.E. The police had come to the same conclusion. His clever deduction had bombed out.

In all probability, Casimir Putch would have remained the big zero among his colleagues if not for a strange twist of fate.

The young reporter developed a painful toothache. Terrified of the dentist, he had gone for days with a swollen jaw and could no longer control the pain with aspirin and ice packs. He made an appointment with Dr. Dan Fieldspin in the Uptown Medical Center. The dentist could squeeze him in at noon, in spite of this being Saturday.

While working on Casimir's mouth, the dentist spoke about the tragedy of his patient, Verna Lake, and her untimely death.

"She had a great tolerance for pain. Unusual for a woman. Never needed novocaine...never complained."

The dentist lifted the air hose from its clip and aimed it at the clean opening in Casimir's tooth. "Too bad. She was so young"

Dr. Fieldspin took an impression of Caz's mouth and told him to return in two weeks for his gold inlay.

While the dentist was doing all this talking about Verna, Casimir's story was rising like a phoenix from the ashes. If the murder victim had been Dr. Fieldspin's patient, surely her records were on file in this office.

Feigning slight fatigue after his dental ordeal, Caz asked if he might rest in the office for a few minutes. The dentist was eager to leave for his tennis match at the club, and told Caz to just flip the door lock when he was ready to go.

In moments, Caz was bending over the file cabinet, leafing through the manila folders to the L's. There it was. Lake, Verna. The folder contained some mouth x-rays, a brief note about recent check-ups and prophylaxis, and a billing history. A small red asterisk drew his eye to the bottom of the billing card; the notation read, "See file for V.Fitch."

Ten minutes later, Caz was walking on air. Even his toothache had disappeared.

"Nice of you to see me, Chief." Caz stood against the brick wall of the Indian Center gym, looking, he hoped, just like Dirty Harry. "This won't take long. Let's you and me talk."

George bristled. "You see my kids waiting there? You can't interrupt their game. Talk about what?"

"Well now," Caz said, settling deeper into his role, "I hear you knew Verna Lake real well. I have some information about her that is real interesting. Thought we might work a deal."

George Burning Tree stood motionless. Not a muscle moved. Not an eyelid twitched. "I don't work deals."

"Yeah, but I know different. You deal plenty with the cops."

George fixed a stony glare on this pitiable excuse for a man, this ridiculous stick with the big pimple ready to pop on his nose, trying to act important.

"I have nothing to say." He turned his back on Caz and walked away.

"How about this, Chief," Caz yelled. "Your pretty girl, Verna, had a cock once!"

George wheeled around so fast that Caz didn't even see the brown fist coming at him, slamming into his face, his gut, his groin, shredding the Dirty Harry image into so much torn and discarded film. Caz fell, rolling on his knees, groaning, his hands clutched between his legs. His glasses had been knocked off, and from where he lay on the floor, all Caz could see was a blurred vision of a pair of huge white Adidas standing next to his face.

❧ EIGHTEEN

Since her encounter with Lieutenant Beltz earlier in the day, Ellie Markham had been distracted and jumpy. She wanted a drink, but would wait until Bob returned. Then she would make a nice icy pitcher of manhattans just the way he liked them. No fruit, no garnish of any kind. Just a healthy shot of bourbon and mix.

She fiddled around in the gallery rearranging the pictures on two walls, then went into the kitchen, took a casserole of beef bourgignon out of the freezer, and set it on a low flame. It would be perfect in time for dinner.

Dusk had fallen, turning the apartment dark and lonely. Funny, with winter coming on, how the lake was losing its blue color. Everything, the water, the grass, the sky, was turning gray. She walked into the den, switched on a lamp next to the sofa, and sat down to watch the five o'clock news. She only half listened. Even as she heard the usual local stories of city hall sleaze and the Bears' scores, her mind wandered back to Beltz and his strange visit. The way he had dropped in and made himself at home. What did he want? Why had he come? Did he know what others had been hinting at? Bob and some blonde fooling around? Since when was gossip police business?

She was brought up short by the announcer's voice as he reported new details on the Uptown murder.

"Police today have revealed that the recent homicide victim, twenty-four-year-old Verna Lake, whose body was found in Uptown earlier this week, was actually a transsexual once known as Verne Fitch. Fitch was a rising young artist who was a graduate of Chicago's Art Institute and had achieved some recent success in the art world. The shocking development of this double life is leading the police into a more extensive investigation of this bizarre murder."

Ellie shook with a sudden chill. In a flash, as clear as if he stood before her, she saw his face in the garden the day they met. It was a painful vision, disquieting, so real she almost reached out to touch him. That the innocent and charming young boy with the enormous talent and potential for greatness should, by an utterly mad mutilation, have turned into a cheap tramp was an absurdity too outrageous to comprehend. That he was also carrying on an affair with her husband, was the blackest of black jokes.

The measure of her grief was so great, Ellie could not sit still. She jumped off the couch and began to pace the room nervously, bumping into furniture and crying aloud, "Oh, my Verne, my talented Verne."

"Where are you, Ellie?" Bob called from the foyer. "Is that really beef bourgignon I smell?"

The living room was dark, but from the light spilling into the hall, he assumed she was in the den. Silly voices and canned laughter grew louder as he entered the room.

"You deaf, Ellie?" he asked good-naturedly as he flipped off the blaring Three Stooges comedy that had followed the news.

Ellie didn't look up. Her voice, when she spoke, came to him from a cold grave. "It was all your fault."

"What was all my fault? What's the matter with you?"

"I know about it, Bob. I know about Verna."

He stiffened. Hollow-eyed and suddenly old, he sank

heavily into an arm chair. "Jesus!"

The room was cold and silent. The one lamp shone a puddle of light at their feet, leaving the rest of the room in darkness.

"How could you have done this to me?" Ellie said miserably.

Bob sat like a stone, wanting desperately to say the right words, but nothing clever or flip came to mind. How do you justify infidelity.

"It happened, Ellie, but it's over."

"I know it's over."

He looked up at her, hang-dog, penitent. "How did you find out?"

Her voice dripped with sarcasm. "I just heard it on the news."

"The news? My God, what did they say about me?" His face was a pasty white. "Ellie, tell me what they said about me."

"Why you? Why are you so concerned about you?" Her brows drew together in a questioning frown. "There was a detective here today. Does he think you had something to do with it?"

"Goddam it, Ellie! What's going on here?" he shouted. "What detective?"

His neat polished exterior had suddenly shattered, falling in pieces as she watched.

He seized her shoulders and shook her violently. "What detective? When was he here?"

She wrenched free. "This afternoon," she cried, "and take your hands off me!"

"What did he want to know? What did he ask you?"

"He wanted to see *you*, to talk to *you*. I realize that now. But he asked me questions. About…Verna Lake."

Bob turned from her, shoulders sagging, suddenly calm and resigned. "So they know."

"So do I, NOW! The whole world knows, Bob. It was all right there in glorious color…on the five o'clock news."

He turned back, confused, wondering if they were on the same wave length. "The murder?"

It was Ellie's turn to be disconcerted, perplexed at the twists and turns in this baffling dialogue. "That's only part of it," she said in a choked voice, "there's more, darling husband, much more. Were you aware that your bed partner was once upon a time a male? A man. And not just a man. Verna Lake was…was…oh, God…Verna Lake was Verne Fitch! My own…"

Ellie dissolved in a heap to the floor, tears streaming down her face.

Bob stared at her in disbelief, then ran, gagging and retching, to the bathroom.

❧ NINETEEN

In sorrow thou shalt bring forth children, May Fitch said to herself, as she carefully folded and packed her son's lacy lingerie. Filmy nightgowns in pinks and creamy ivories, and garter belts with matching bras, all handled reverently, as if folding the shroud of Turin.

She and Carl had arrived at Pearl Minkoff's that morning from Fort Wayne. The police had informed them they could now pick up Verna's personal effects. These same police were having difficulty using the correct terminology when speaking to the Fitches about the victim. Should they say daughter? or son? Verne or Verna? There was a hesitancy, a reluctance to hurt them. So they said victim, hoping that was neutral enough.

Carl sat on a folding chair, turning the leaves of Verne's art portfolio. His face reflected a mixed feeling of sorrow and squeamishness at handling the strange assortment of pictures.

Some were familiar. He remembered Verne working on them during his high school years. Funny caricatures of friends, a tender portrait of Tom before the tractor accident, a whimsical drawing of their fat old sow Dimples, wearing a ruffled bonnet and a garter belt holding up black stockings. He passed by that one quickly and found himself staring at a charcoal rendering of the old shed behind their house, which should have been torn down years ago. He had known then it was never good for much except storing old used tires and worn furniture, like the hand-made cradle he'd fashioned lovingly for Verne. They would never use it again. May had made that quite clear. But she never let him throw it out.

"Decide now on the paintings you want, Carl," May said, closing the bottom drawer of the bureau. "The rest we'll try to sell."

He shrugged. "I only want the ones of the farm. I don't understand the others."

"Don't be silly. We have no idea what they're worth."

"That all you can think of? The money?" he said sharply.

"No sense giving it away." She lifted her face in a righteous pose. "St. Luke said the rich man fares sumptuously every day."

"Yeah, well, if you eat too much you can choke to death."

He snapped shut the portfolio and fastened the strap around it. "Are you done yet? I can't sit here any more."

"No, I still have the closet and some things in the medicine chest. If you want to go, go ahead. I can finish by myself."

He hefted the portfolio. "I'll take this down to the truck and wait for you. Try to hurry it up."

May sighed and turned back to her task. She never thought for a minute that Verne ever wore any of this. There must be some mistake about the clothes.

She took down the dresses from the closet rod and folded them neatly in the box. Next, the blouses and slacks, high-heeled pumps and flat sandals. There were small purses in various colors with shoulder straps, and a silk-lined raincoat.

As she packed, she couldn't help wondering how much the paintings were really worth. Could Verne have bought all this from only the sale of his paintings? Or was there money coming in from someplace else. May veered quickly away from that thought and reached for the box on the top shelf.

113

Her foot slipped on the rickety stool and the box fell, scattering its contents on the floor.

She kneeled and began scooping up the old photographs and mementos from Verne's youth. One thing caught her eye. The small box that held the Cross pen and pencil set she and Carl had given their son last Christmas.

Tenderly she opened the box and stared at the engraving, for which she had paid an extra five dollars. Verne Fitch. "Verne Fitch," she said aloud, as if willing that in the very mention of his name, he would exist again.

That had been a wonderful Christmas, Verne full of anecdotes and jokes about the big city, his friends, and the good times they had together. He smiled a lot and hummed bits of Broadway tunes, even imitating the popular singers, pretending to sing when the radio played the songs.

And he had looked so handsome in his new city clothes, nice sportcoat, designer ties. She had noticed the label on a tie tossed on a chair one day, and had smiled at her son's taste. Paris France, no less. She had tweaked him about it, and he had tried to teach her the correct pronunciation of Givenchy.

He hadn't gone out much that weekend. Stayed close to home, played checkers with his dad and watched television. Verne was more interested in The Nutcracker with Baryshnikov, while Carl wanted to see the Bears' game. She had roasted a turkey and baked Verne's favorite pumpkin pie. And he hadn't even objected too much when she insisted on reading from Isaiah before dinner, the portion sung by the chorus in Handel's Messiah.

They had exchanged gifts afterwards. In his new jovial manner, which she had attributed to his new life in Chicago, he had stuck cotton on his chin, donned a red stocking cap, and played Santa Claus.

She had thought then how much he had changed since first leaving home. Her quiet shy boy had been transformed into a sophisticated man about town. She had been so proud he had finally come out of his shell, in spite of Carl's dour mutterings.

The only sour note in the whole weekend was his anger when she tried to take his measurements for a sweater she planned knitting for him.

"No," he had snapped, backing away.

"Verne, my goodness, it has to fit. Stand still...I need to measure your chest."

"I'll get you one of my old sweaters," he said, rushing from the room.

He had been clever, all right. There was no way she could have known. How dare he come home putting on this despicable act in front of his parents. What an abomination he had become.

May closed her eyes and intoned softly, "Be sober, be vigilant; because the devil walketh about seeking whom he may devour."

It was a tricky three days, that Christmas vacation, the juxtaposition of the shy, introverted male son, Verne, with the new flamboyant persona of Verna. A careful monitoring of every word and gesture was required to pull it off; it was an anxious and tense time.

Verne/Verna had made a valiant effort to control a growing irritation with his/her parents that weekend at home, using the utmost self-restraint when May wanted measurements for a sweater. All hell would break loose if she were to feel the rounded upturned breasts that were hopefully hidden under a bulky shirt.

Verne had not seen his parents since the operation. Verna had kept up her correspondence with them as their son, and the pretense was carried out with the help of the P.O. Box, never quite explained to May's satisfaction.

It had been a study in deceit. The masquerade of affection, the obvious relishing of the food May had prepared especially for her son, which was never enjoyed to the degree May had built up in her own mind. Worst of all were the men's clothes, so uncomfortable and foreign to the soft new body wearing them. Fortunately, Verne had worn his blond hair longish, much to his mother's irritation, during high school, and now, with the beautiful blonde page-boy trimmed to a more masculine length, the deception was complete.

Lying in the old bed at night, remnants of life-long disatisfactions returned: the hated masculine body in which all those feminine thoughts were imprisoned, the agony of appearing one way to the world, when deep in his heart, his very soul, he knew he was just the opposite. This was a bad time.

Thank God the sham was over. Except for the family. How long could it be this way; the truth will have to come out one day.

His move to the big city had been lucky. Chicago was big enough to absorb Verne and his problem, and ultimately lead him to a solution. And too, the preparation for the surgery, all done while attending art school, could be accomplished without anyone close to him knowing about it.

It didn't take long to agree to the steps required before the final change. Every cent he earned and borrowed went to the team of psychiatrists, psychologists, gynecologists, plastic surgeons, urologists, and endocrinologists that had to be consulted. Legal and religious professionals also entered the picture. Criteria had to be met by the candidate to the satisfaction of the medical crew, which included months and months of shots and follow-up consultations. Plus the acting-out by cross-dressing, insisted upon by the psychiatric group. Play the part, determine how comfortable you are in the desired role.

And that wasn't easy. Like the first venturing forth in high heels, teetering across Halsted Street to Umberto's, watching the trendy singles pair off near the bar.

In summer, the front half of the restaurant was al fresco, and it was here that lonely singles met and made clever conversation, hoping to lead to something more meaningful. Attired in a dirndl, demure linen blouse and full make-up, he had looked as appealing as any of the girls at the bar.

A young executive type, still dressed in his office suit, approached Verne as he sat alone at one of the tables.

"Mind if I join you?" he had asked, smiling pleasantly.

The knot in Verne's stomach had tightened. "No...yes.... sure," he had replied.

"What are you drinking?" the young man asked.

"Rum and coke."

"My folks used to call that a Cuba Libra. You really like it?"

"It goes down real easy," Verne said, "and I'm not much of a drinker."

The young man sat down and lit a cigarette. "My name's Steve."

Verne had a moment of panic. He'd never thought of a name, a new name.

"And yours?" Steve prodded.

"Mine?" With no time to think now, Verne said, "Uh...uh...Vern...Verna."

After a few more minutes of small talk, the knot in Verne's stomach felt like a fist moving up to his throat. He was sweating profusely, sure his make-up was going to streak. It was time to split.

"You must excuse me," he said, glancing at his watch. "I'm late for an appointment."

He had run, making an ungainly exit in the high heels, praying he wouldn't trip.

After that, it had been easier. He found these mandatory excursions into make-believe land taking on a more comfortable posture. He actually began to grow into the part, feeling more like the woman he was pretending to be, knew he was inside. It wasn't second nature; he had been cheated at birth with the wrong set of reproductive organs. And he was angry at the wasted years imprisoned in the wrong body.

When looking in a mirror, he saw how, with hormones, the skin had undergone dramatic change in softness and texture, the electrolysis erasing all testimony of a beard. When he stroked his own cheek, he understood from his new androgynous insight, what a turn-on this could be to the male. His hips were rounder, his waist more indented, his nipples more prominent and tender.

At the same time, he was discovering an unpleasant side effect. He was losing his clout. As a female, he was no longer a first class citizen. Clerks snubbed him, waiters patronized him. He was painfully aware that his new sex was, in some milieus, invisible.

Even so, it would be worth it. There were unanticipated advantages. The attentions from men, chairs held, doors opened, heavy paintings carried, were a delightful new experience.

As the months of medical and psychiatric therapy progressed, Verne's enthusiasm blossomed to the point where he could never again revert to his male existence. He was a woman, and by God, there was no question he would go through with the surgery.

That he fooled his parents so completely was another gift from Santa. There was no indication they even suspected any change in their son. Carl had always been distant, and had showed no interest in his son's new life in Chicago. Now, in games of checkers during the Christmas visit, there was a new friendliness, an openness never manifest before.

May was something else. She still ranted her biblical exhortations, like that ridiculous Messiah bit before dinner. What self-control; not a peep out of Verne/Verna. The model child. For these few days at least. There were evasive responses to May's ill-disguised queries about where her son lived, his friends, his work, and when she hinted about visits, he quickly discouraged her. However, he did tell her he had a room in Mrs. Minkoff's house, but he might not stay there for long. She should continue to use the P.O. box number.

His anxiety grew in Fort Wayne, and when he bid them goodbye, he sighed with relief. Verne threw a kiss to his parents, climbed into his car, and Verna returned to Chicago.

⅔ TWENTY

That Sunday night it was apparent to both Beltz and Molly that they had different ideas about food. Except for Chinese. When they started to argue about Mandarin versus Cantonese, Molly had thrown her hands up, and cried, "Anywhere!"

Ralph Chung's Chinese Smorgasbord was on Lakeview, across from the flower conservatory in Lincoln Park. Beltz knew it from years past, but when they walked in, he hadn't remembered how dark it was. So, he shrugged, they're all dark.

They drank their first martinis under dusty paper lanterns that gave little light. Molly told Stanley to order.

When tea came, he bluntly asked, "What's with that rose you always wear?"

"This?" Molly said, touching the faded silk petals. "Popeye wore it on a ribbon around his neck."

"Popeye?"

Molly gave an involuntary sigh and told Beltz all about her marriage, Sky, and everything that died with him. She also told him the truth, that she was a photographer, and that she was not writing a book. She explained that it was her search for props that resulted in finding the hand. "Anyway," she added wistfully, "I can't seem to let go of this poor rose."

"Did you have to lie?" he asked.

"Would you have told me anything if I hadn't?"

"I don't know."

"See?"

When he didn't answer, she turned to another subject. "So, I'm the last to know. Seems ironic to me. The one to find the body, well, at least part of it, is the last to hear the truth."

"Don't get huffy now," Beltz said.

"How long have you known she was a transsexual?"

"Since we found the body."

"And the papers? How did you keep it out of the news with all those reporters hanging around?"

"It wasn't easy."

"Why did you keep it quiet?"

The waiter brought large bowls of shrimp in lobster sauce and sweet and sour duck. He spooned steaming rice on their plates and then moved silently away, disappearing into the kitchen.

"Why did you keep it quiet?" Molly repeated.

"Because if we divulged all the facts to the public, we'd never stand a chance. Don't forget, we get lots of leads from informers, and they're not too eager to be exposed."

"Like the Chief," Molly said smugly.

"Mrs. Fast, how clever! How did you know about him?" Beltz's eyes twinkled.

Molly took a bite of shrimp and said, "I'm not stupid. I know a can opener isn't a key to the john. Mm-mm, this is delicious. So, spending time in your station, although a bit hinky, paid off. I know the Chief personally."

He looked up, surprised. "How did that happen?"

"I just went to see him. He's cranky, but if you handle him right..."

"Oh-ho! You are turning into a first-class meddler. Next thing, you'll want a shield."

Molly laughed. "I could have used one that day. And I don't mean to interfere, although I really think I'm getting to be quite good at it." Her smile faded. "I often wonder if the police work as diligently to solve a murder like this. Are they as sympathetic as they would be if the victim were a prominent member of the community?"

Beltz's expression clouded over. "All murders are important. We don't measure our diligence by the prominence of the victim. I hope this isn't a common misconception in the public's mind. But then, we've never had good press."

Molly shattered the quiet with a piercing scream and jumped up on her chair. "Get it out of here!" she yelled.

Confused, Beltz looked under the table, certain he'd find a little mouse. Instead, a small long-haired calico cat sat cleaning its paws. He looked up at Molly, who stood shaking with fright.

"Get that damn cat out of here!" she shrieked.

By this time, the waiter came running, bowed apologetically to Beltz and Molly, picked up the cat by its neck, and padded silently out.

"That was some performance. They scare you that much?" Beltz asked, helping her down.

"I hate them! I hate cats. They scare me to death."

"I can tell. Probably the owner's pet. I'll bet you scared him more than he scared you." Molly drained her martini glass and raised her big eyes to Beltz. "I know it's irrational, but I can't help it."

"Not at all. It's a full-blown phobia...even has a name—ailurophobia."

"Phobia—schmobia. I don't care what it's called...cats have terrified me all my life. But let's forget it. And I apologize if I embarrassed you."

After a few moments to catch her breath, Molly said, "About this transsexual thing...why do they do it?"

"Hard to say. Each one has a different reason."

"For instance?"

"I don't know. I've never felt that way. I'm perfectly content being what I am." He winked at her. "With all the natural urges, that is."

Molly blushed. She said quickly, "You never told me what you thought about Bob's wife. Do you think she knew about his affair?"

"Wives have a way of knowing about their husband's indiscretions," he commented airily.

"I thought wives were always the last to know."

"Well, considering that bracelet and the brazen inscription…he couldn't have been trying too hard to conceal his actions. Maybe he wanted her to find out. Who knows?" He handed her the dish of duck. It was almost empty. "Have some more."

"Don't mind if I do. It's good."

Beltz laughed. "But in an hour, you'll be hungry again."

"And so will you. Stanley…?"

"Molly…?"

"Tell me about Ellie Markham."

He licked around the spoon for the last drop of rice. "Personally, I think she's a stuck-up eastern snob, absolutely devoid of charm and humor. Dull. And her husband probably had good reason to stray."

"That's very sexist!"

"All I said was she would turn off most men. A woman doesn't have to be beautiful. But she has to give off some kind of aura, some positive vibes. The most appealing woman I ever knew was, feature for feature, quite homely. And not young, by the way. But she could charm the pants off me."

Molly's blue eyes widened. "Did she?"

"Let's get back to your original question. Ellie Markham didn't fool me. She knew."

"Is she a suspect?"

"The only thing I'm sure of right now is that being with

you today has been, in spite of the cat, the best thing that's happened to me in a long time."

"I'd be annoyed at your obvious and evasive tactics, Lieutenant Beltz, if it weren't for the fact that I am so very flattered."

He sat back and looked at her for a moment. "See? Now that's charm."

"You're right on time, Detective Beltz," Bob Markham said, opening his apartment door Monday afternoon. "Come in. Can I fix you a drink?"

"No, thank you. I don't drink on duty," Beltz said, glancing out the window. "I'll never get over this view. I don't think I'd ever leave this apartment if I lived here."

"You get tired of it," Bob observed, "especially in winter when there aren't any boats to watch. Sometimes, this high up, we're completely enveloped in clouds. It can be eerie."

Beltz made no comment. But he did see that Molly had been right on the mark; this guy looked just like Pearl's description.

"What is it you wanted to see me about?" Bob asked.

"I suppose you know now about the homicide victim in Uptown? Verna Lake?"

"I heard about it, yes, on the news."

"Did you know her?"

"Why would you think I knew her?"

"We know that she was an accomplished artist, and you being in the business and all, well, I thought there might be a connection."

Bob took time to fill his pipe with tobacco, tamp it down, then light it. After drawing deeply, he asked, "Is that all you have?"

Markham's pipe had gone out. Without looking at Beltz he relit it and said, "What would I be doing with a transsexual? The mere thought of it is repulsive."

"If you didn't know she was a transsexual," Beltz said softly, "until you heard it on the news, it wouldn't be quite so repulsive, would it."

"Didn't my wife answer all your questions?"

"How could she?"

Markham busied himself reaming the pipe bowl, then added more tobacco. Beltz waited patiently.

"Lieutenant Beltz..." Markham said, "by the way, do I call you detective? Or Mister?"

"Either one."

"Well then, Mister. The news did say she was a transsexual."

"I'm sure you can tell me more, Mr. Markham."

"So...I knew her. So what?"

"How well did you know her?"

"Well, I didn't know her as Verna. I knew her as Verne Fitch." Markham juggled the two identities, trying to keep repugnance out of his voice. "He was one of our artists working on an exclusive contract. A very talented young man. Had a big future in front of him. Can't for the life of me get used to the fact that he changed his sex. I mean it blows my mind."

"So you knew her only when she was Verne Fitch. You never knew her as Verna Lake?"

"I might have met her at some showing, not realizing it was the same person," Bob said off-handedly.

"Then do I understand you correctly? You never knew a Verna Lake, whether she was once Verne Fitch or not."

"Correct."

"Tell me then, Sir. Does 418 Kenmore Avenue mean anything to you?"

"No."

"Did you ever visit anyone at that address?"

"No."

"In other words, you don't know anybody who has lived there or lives there now?"

"How many times do I have to tell you? No. No. NO!"

Beltz watched Markham worrying his thumb against his

finger, the sound almost like a lapstrake boat against a pier tire. His eyes never left the detective's face and the pipe was forgotten.

Beltz smiled pleasantly. "You ever been to a jeweler on north Clark…?"

"No."

"…called Nick's Uptown Jewelers?"

"No."

"I think you're lying, Mr. Markham."

"The hell I am."

"You any good with quotations, Mr. Markham?"

"It depends. Maybe something famous, like the Gettysburg Address."

Beltz took a crumpled piece of paper from his pocket. "Help me with this, if you can. 'A lover without indiscretion is no lover at all.' It's driving me crazy, where it's from."

Markham answered quickly, too quickly. "Never heard it."

"That right? We have a witness that says differently."

"Bull shit! You trying to trap me or something? Those words don't mean a God damn thing to me."

"Well, it seems this witness claims you know this quotation real well. He'll swear it under oath."

A muscle near Markham's eye began to twitch. "You've got nothing to go on. Nothing! If all you've got is some damn bracelet…oh, God!"

Beltz crumpled the paper and stuck it back in his pocket. "You want to call your lawyer, Mr. Markham?" he said evenly,"or shall we go down to the station.?"

Markham seemed overwhelmed. "I don't need my lawyer, and I don't want to go to any station." He sighed. "Can't we talk here? I'll tell you as much as I know."

"That would be a great help," Beltz said. "Do you want to light your pipe again, Mr. Markham?"

"No. But I'd like some coffee. Surely that's not against the rules."

"Not at all. I'll take mine black."

Markham walked with a heavy step into the kitchen and filled the percolator with water and grounds, plugged it in, and drank a large glass of ice water. His throat was dry, his lips cracked and white.

He closed his eyes, thinking ironically that he had never allowed a thought of Verna to intrude into his home setting. And here she was, as big as life, or death, sitting there grinning, the same way she had grinned the last time they were together.

He remembered how she had opened the apartment door and posed, back-lit by a soft lamp, so that he could see her naked silhouette under the sheer lavender negligée. No matter how firm his resolve coming up the stairs, it was forgotten with his instant erection. He caught her around the waist and pulled her close.

"Well," she had said, in that husky stirring voice, "can't you say hello first?"

"This is my hello." He nibbled at the lobe of one ear and worked his hands under her breasts. At the same time, her hand caressed his erection through the cloth of his trousers and she said, laughing, "It's a good thing we don't meet in public...what a sight! We'd be arrested for lewd and crude behavior."

"If you don't let go," Bob protested, breathing heavily, "the evening will be considerably shortened."

"I'm not worried about that. After all, haven't you called me Lazarus more than once? I can always raise you from the dead."

"Don't I know it." He watched her move away, so graceful and so sure that his eyes were following her. She was a beautiful girl. Small and delicate, the personification of feminine allure. Even her slender hands, in spite of the long, garishly painted finger nails, made fluid motions as she punctuated her remarks and moved like a dancer across a stage. She lowered her lashes under his steady gaze and after these many times together, he recognized the preliminary to the scene that always followed.

She was seated on the bed, crossing and uncrossing her long slim legs, the tantalizing movement calculated and precise.

"You didn't even notice my new rug," she said peevishly. "It's soft. Come. Try it."

His eyes moved to the fluffy white oval in front of the fireplace. The gas flame, red and blue and never changing, warmed the room. He tried to shake off the cynical thought interfering with the erotic setting: how much was this new acquisition going to cost him?

Verna held out her hand and pulled him down with her to the enveloping softness of the white rug.

"I've never seen this tie," she said, playfully undoing the windsor knot. "There's so much about you that I don't get to see...that I'm not a part of."

She kept talking all the while she undressed him, the words seductive and titillating. "For someone who doesn't work out, you're in great shape. So hard. I can't even squeeze that inch." She pinched him at the waist.

He pulled her hands away. "You don't think this is a workout? I must lose a couple of pounds each time I see you."

"Is my poor Bobby tired when he goes home?" She leaned over and kissed him, her tongue licking at his smooth lips, then darting between them, exploring. He responded to her as always, eagerly, transported into the inevitable surge of passion he had never felt before knowing her. Senses previously untapped were discovered and brought, exploding, to life here in this room, and he knew all these feelings, while genuine, had nothing to do with reason. It didn't matter. Nothing mattered except joining with her in this weekly visit to Eden.

Slowly he undid the three small buttons holding her negligée and she lay naked before him. Her soft white skin glowed in the firelight, accentuating the perfection of her body and the small triangle of blonde hair.

She rolled over and began licking at his body, slowly, teasing him with her tongue on the inside of his legs, across his penis, flicking it with quick feathery strokes that made him moan and cry for more.

"Take it in your mouth, Verna, all the way, all the way."

She did, sucking, pulling the skin up and down, her clever tongue never still, lightly lingering on the top, then taking it deep into her throat.

He began thrusting his pelvis, slowly, her mouth tight, holding him inside until he could feel his seed rising.

He moaned and pulled out quickly, turning himself around to kiss her.

"Touch me where I like it, Bob," she said softly, "you know where I like it. There. There! Oh yes, more, do it, do it!"

Verna turned so that one breast rested near his mouth. He eagerly nursed at it, her small mewling sounds feeding his desire. His hand worked between her legs and she uttered a little cry and pulled him into her.

It was over quickly. Bob shuddered and climaxed as Verna cried his name aloud, her long nails digging into his back.

Later, lying together before the fire, Bob touched the raw spots she had inflicted and asked, "When are you going to cut those damn nails?"

"Why? Did your wife say something?"

"Don't be silly."

"I didn't bring it up."

"Let's drop it."

"If you really think it's that important, I'll trim them down. After all," she said in a little baby voice, "I want to please you."

"That would be nice. By the way, how much did the rug cost?"

"Honey, it didn't cost much. Only a hundred and twenty-five on sale. It's Peruvian. And you know how bare this room was."

Damn. With the rent and all, that brings the monthly tab to close to six-hundred dollars. How long could he keep this up? "Listen, Verna, you're going to have to show some restraint. I'm not a rich man."

She began humming "If I Were a Rich Man," and this only aggravated him further. He was suddenly uneasy with her and her lack of sensitivity. With the passion gone and forgotten, the hard fact of their relationship began to cloy.

He stood and dressed. "It's late."

She was surprised. "Bob, you're not leaving yet."

"Yes...I'm having trouble with this one-sided conversation." His voice was brittle, tense.

"Why are you so angry? What did I say?"

"It's obvious you don't care how you spend my money. Perhaps what you need is someone in the options market to keep you in the style you prefer. I can't do it."

"You've never nagged at me about money," Verna said, raising her voice. Anger caused a startling change in her expression. Bob had seen it happen before, the brittle, almost synthetic glaze spreading over her features, and for a brief moment, she seemed old and ignoble.

He turned away. "Let's forget it."

"No, let's have it out. I suppose you begrudge the wine you drank, and the lamp I bought last month that, as you so gallantly said then, 'highlights the gold in my hair,' she hissed. "And this..."

She crossed to the dresser and picked up a red snakeskin wallet. "Take it!" She threw it at him. "You paid for it!"

"Verna..."

"And this..." She tossed the negligée. It fell short and landed in a lavender heap at his feet. She was darting around the room, her usual seductive rhythm lost in anger, throwing clothing, books, magazines in her fury. She was naked, and he thought how ridiculous she looked, almost like an adolescent boy when denied the use of the car.

She stopped abruptly and undid the clasp of the bracelet she wore. "Take this too...and stick it!"

The bracelet grazed his head and fell with a clank to the floor. He stared at her, knowing he'd been with her for the last time. Then he turned, walked out, and slammed the door.

The coffee pot was perking, and Markham was brought back to the present. He filled the tray and returned to the living room.

Beltz held the steaming mug and sipped the coffee. "Tell me about Verna."

"I loved her. I really did. It's hard to explain, but she got to me...Ellie and I have been happily married for nine years, but she never made me feel like Verna did."

Beltz had no trouble with that statement, after talking with Ellie yesterday. "How did you meet?"

"At the opera. It was strange. Ellie had a cold so I had this extra ticket. I called the box office earlier, and told them to sell the seat if they could. It's a tax deduction, you know. When I arrived that night, Verna was sitting in Ellie's seat. We spoke of other performances of the opera, The Barber of Seville, comparing them to this one, and I asked her out for a drink afterwards. Knowing about her now, it seems so ghoulish, how she fooled me. It's amazing what modern science has accomplished. Or maybe I shouldn't call this an accomplishment." He looked at Beltz. "Don't you think?"

"Please continue."

"There's not much more to tell. We saw each other once a week. I took care of her expenses. It was one of those things."

"But your wife found out."

"No, not then. It was after I decided not to see her again."

"Can you be sure?"

"I know my wife, Lieutenant. Her anger yesterday was real. She would have said something before if she had known. I guess I have you to thank for that."

"Why did you and Verna break up? That is, assuming you're telling the truth about not seeing her again. And when was this?"

Markham refilled their mugs. "You can be sure I'm telling you the truth now. I have to say it's a relief. To get it all out."

"When did you stop seeing her?"

"She was getting greedy and possessive. I couldn't handle it. This was my first affair, believe it or not. It was the only thing I could think of to do...take off. When was it?" He glanced at his watch. "Two weeks ago today, to be exact. I went there on Monday nights."

Beltz sat hunched in the chair. He shook his head. "You know, it's still difficult for me to believe that you couldn't tell this woman was once a man. I mean, you had intercourse with her, you must have done other things to her...wasn't she...different?"

"Christ!" Markham exploded, "I threw up for an hour yesterday when I found out. I haven't closed my eyes..."

"You've been fucking her for a couple of months, paying her freight, and all of a sudden, one week before she's murdered, you decide to break up. Now isn't that convenient!"

Markham rose and stood over Beltz. "Listen here, Lieutenant, I volunteered this information. I didn't have to answer your goddam questions, and without an attorney. I've told the truth. If you think I killed her, you're out of your tree! I loved her. Then I didn't love her. But I didn't kill her."

Beltz ignored the outburst. "And you had no idea this apparent woman was Verne Fitch, the male artist you had under exclusive contract?"

"Absolutely not. I never met Fitch. Ellie was the one who signed him up."

"And you never wondered about all those paintings and sketches in her portfolio?"

"What portfolio?" Markham looked genuinely surprised.

Beltz's eyes hardened. He was nose to nose with his suspect. "You didn't see the charcoal sketch hanging on the back of her bedroom door?"

"Lieutenant Beltz, there was nothing hanging on the back of the bedroom door the last time I saw Verna Lake."

❧ TWENTY-ONE

Casimir Putch had remained in St. Phillipi's Sunday night after his run-in with the Chief, but Monday night found him back at Area Three Headquarters. For once he was going to be the center of attention. No way was he going to let George Burning Tree get away with such a savage and unprovoked attack. He would have been killed by that big moronic hulk if the boys on the basketball team had not pulled him off.

He looked like a war casualty; his head swathed in bandages, his right arm in a sling and one side of his jaw swollen out of shape. Even though his lips were stitched, and both eyes blackened, his appearance was better than usual. So much of what was wrong with Caz was covered up. Like a neat spread pulled over an unmade bed.

The cops started in on him almost immediately.

"What'sa matter, Caz, he use a tomahawk on you?"

"Hey Caz, you have your hands tied behind your back?"

"You bought it boy. Indian one…Noodle nothing."

"You still got your scalp, Caz?"

Laughter shook the room.

Casimir was surprised. He'd expected accolades, at least compassion for the beating he had taken. But his thinking was way out of line. After all the jokes and teasing, underneath it all, they were angry. Angry he had taken it upon himself in the guise of crime reporter to question, without permission, a prime suspect in a murder investigation. He would blow it for all of them. They let him know, in not too delicate terms, that if he ever repeated it he could go squeeze his pimples somewhere else.

The charge against George had been reduced from attempted murder to aggravated battery. His public defender had done a good job in court that morning. Once the judge had all the facts, George Burning Tree was released on bail.

So much for Caz. He was always in the middle of a rainstorm when the sun was shining.

The Chief went directly from court to work at the moving company and from there to the Indian Center. He was coaching his boys on dribbling when Beltz walked in. With Molly.

Beltz had left her at the door to the gym with strict instructions to sit down and not move from the chair. He wasn't happy about her being here at all. In fact, how he even found himself in this situation, babysitting a grown woman with a penchant for amateur sleuthing, was beyond his reason.

She had phoned him earlier in the day, looking for a set of handcuffs. She had this great idea for a picture—she wouldn't go into it now—but could she borrow a pair from the station, she had asked sweetly.

He could almost visualize her fluttering eyelashes as she spoke to him on the phone, the image not unpleasant, and he found himself agreeing to meet her at the Center. But she had to promise to be quiet, only to be seen and not heard.

"Just a couple of questions, Chief, if you don't mind," Beltz said

"No. I'm too busy."

"Chief, it's important we talk."

"I told you everything," George said, still demonstrating the art of dribbling to a few of the younger boys.

"I hate to take you away from your kids, but we can go down to the station if you prefer."

133

The dribbling stopped. The boys took the ball and drifted away and George regarded the detective with irritation.

"Shit," he said. "What the hell else do you want from me?"

"One more thing. It's about a drawing, a charcoal drawing that I found on the back of Verna's bedroom door. Did you happen to see it the last time you were with her?"

The Chief didn't answer. Instead, he looked straight ahead at Molly sitting off in a corner, and the briefest touch of a smile crossed his face. "That lady over there...she with you?"

Beltz followed his eyes, puzzled. "Yeah, she's waiting for me. Why?"

"I'll talk to her."

Beltz couldn't figure it, but if satisfying this whim of the Chief's would answer his question, he would go along with it. He waved Molly over.

She approached, her blue eyes wide with curiosity.

"I want to thank you, Mrs. Molly Fast, for helping fix my net. You should not call it the loop stitch. It should be called the Fast stitch."

"I'll take out a patent," Molly said, beaming.

Beltz wondered what the hell was going on.

"Important things first, Lieutenant. I had to thank this lady for her help. Now I'll answer your question. No, I did not see anything on the back of Verna's bedroom door last time I was with her. Except a hook. And I hang my shirt on that."

Beltz chewed that over for a minute. "You're sure?"

"Sure."

"Okay. Thanks, Chief. C'mon, Molly." He took her by the arm and led her out of the building, muttering, "Why do I have the feeling, sometimes, that you've just built the bridge I'm crossing?"

They walked outside into the cold evening. The autumn had moved ahead to November third, and it was downright frosty tonight. Molly pulled the collar of her old sheared beaver coat tightly around her face as Beltz started the engine.

"Would you like to explain yourself over a nice martini?" Beltz asked. "All of these little private investigations you've been undertaking? I thought we discussed this before."

His fingers gripped the wheel tighter. He could deal with felons, hardened criminals, shoplifters, arsonists, the worst the street could produce. But this short, soft, curly-haired lady was getting under his skin. He didn't want her around, but he liked her sitting next to him. And she smelled good.

He parked in front of a little bar on Willow Street. Sunset streaked across the western sky, blue and mauve and gold, and Beltz hesitated, looking up. He loved the seasons, especially fall, when the leaves dressed in their vividly colored traveling clothes and left home. It would probably snow before Thanksgiving.

After their drinks were served, Molly said, "Thanks for letting me come along today."

"I had no choice. A stronger man than I could not have resisted that plaintive cry for help."

"You're wondering about the Chief and me, aren't you?"

"I figured since you're so well acquainted with our luxurious surroundings in Uptown, you must know every Indian that wandered in from the reservation." His face was benign, but his tone was as sarcastic as he could muster.

Molly laughed. "You're annoyed with me...again."

She went on to explain her meeting with George. Purely by the merest chance did she happen to hear about him at the station while she was innocently sitting on a bench in those wretched clothes after being mugged by a bag lady and dragged in by two of his patrolmen. After all, she simply had to find out who belonged to that hand that *she* found, didn't she, and didn't she have the right to follow up by going to see George. And big deal, all they talked about was that loop stitch she showed him, which evidently helped him a lot. "Now is that so terrible, Lieutenant Beltz?" she said vehemently, taking a long swallow of her martini.

"Either you're some kind of genius, or you're an accident-prone opportunist. And I can't allow you to be a genius because that's my job. I'll solve the case. You can tag along...sometimes." He finished his drink. "Another one?"

"Why not?" This was the first time Molly was getting a buzz on with another man since Sky's death and it was fun. Somehow, she had the sense that he too was enjoying the scene. He blustered and scolded and teased unmercifully, but there was an underlying affection hovering between his rebukes.

"My very own Miss Marple," Beltz began, "let me run this by you, since you seem to be on speaking terms with all my suspects. Listen, and don't interrupt.

"Verna Lake has existed only since the spring of last year. Before that, she was known as Verne Fitch, a male artist who had sold his paintings to the Markham Art Gallery. It seems that the wife, Ellie Markham, never knew she was receiving additional paintings from the new Verna Lake. And her husband Bob claims he never knew Verna was a transsexual, even though he was sleeping with her. Though I find that hard to believe."

He downed the last of his drink and thoughtfully chewed an olive. "Verna," he continued, "at the same time she was sleeping with Bob Markham, who incidentally was paying her rent, was also fooling around with George Burning Tree, who is known for his vicious and easily provoked temper. He has beaten up a co-worker, slapped Verna around, and yesterday pulverized a reporter who foresaw instant glory by informing George he had been screwing a transsexual.

"Hell hath no fury like a woman scorned and drab Ellie could be hopping mad that her dapper Bob was having an affair. Mad enough to kill? Who knows?

"Charcoal dust was found under the fingernails of the deceased, Verna Lake, who must have done a charcoal drawing shortly before her death. I saw that kind of drawing, a weird phantasm...a nightmare image hanging on the back of her bedroom door, but nobody else claims to have seen it. It was like a hideous illustration from a black sabbath, a diabolical travesty of a wide-eyed prophet of old with outstretched arms scowling down on the congregation.

"And the artist's agent, this Ellie Markham, claims that Verne had ceased to work in that medium. Ergo, why did the artist, male or female, return to that medium in the last few hours of her life? Why? Why?

"I'm always hit by a stampede of whys." He tried to signal the waitress.

"If my assumption is right," he continued, "that drawing now lies in her portfolio that the parents took home. And I've got a hunch. The first thing tomorrow, I'm running down to Fort Wayne." The lines around his eyes deepened as he smiled. "And if you're thinking about it, NO! You can't come with me."

Molly raised her hands innocently. "Who? Me?"

Lieutenant Beltz had no trouble finding the Fitch house from the main road this time. All the leaves had fallen from the surrounding trees, leaving the limbs brown and skeletal against the sky. As he approached the house, the open door of the garage revealed the same messy clutter of odd farm implements and old machinery he had seen on his earlier visit. On this Tuesday morning he noticed the shed visible through the bare branches separating the house from the garage. From where he was standing, he could see Verna's dressing table. The smart little Victorian reproduction was leaning against an old wooden cradle. The picture touched him; a lifetime stretched between those two objects.

He climbed the front steps and pressed the bell. The door opened instantly.

"I'm surprised to see you, Lieutenant Beltz," May Fitch said. "Come in. It's cold."

"I hope I'm not disturbing you."

"I'm almost finished," May said. "Verne's clothes...I packed them in a box. The Salvation Army's picking them up this afternoon. Will you sit down?"

"If I might see the portfolio of paintings that was in your son's apartment, then I won't keep you too long."

"Come with me. It's in the back room."

Beltz followed her through the tidy kitchen into a small room at the rear of the house. It was obviously used as a pantry at one time. Built-in shelves covered one wall, several old suitcases were stacked under the window, but Beltz could not take his eyes from the crucifix hanging on the wall. The vertical piece must have been a yard long. The carved figure of the agonized Jesus pinned to the cross and bleeding profusely from his wounds was an overwhelming sight in that small room. But it would have been shocking anywhere. The blood had been painted a bright crimson, and Beltz had the sudden urge to wipe it off.

"Carl made that," May said, watching the policeman, "when we first married. He didn't want to, but he knew it would please me. After all, the Lord Jesus forgives all sin and gives you eternal life through faith. This is where I come to pray sometimes."

Beltz said nothing. He shifted uneasily from one foot to the other.

The portfolio was under the shelves. "I'll leave you here with the pictures. I can't look at them anymore."

He began to sort them into piles on the floor. The watercolors, the charcoals, black ink cartoons, even a few acrylics Verne/Verna must have experimented with. They were unfinished and not as skillfully rendered as the others.

From the dates under the signatures, the cartoons were old, drawn years ago. The one of President Carter was particularly good, with the large toothy smile that almost said "Y'ALL." All the work was outstanding. As he studied each one, a thought began to buzz around in his mind, but he couldn't catch hold of it.

He went back to the quiet and serene pastels of seascapes and open meadows in full bloom, a splash of flowers and a family of white geese in flight.

He turned to the stack of charcoal drawings and began to search for the one he had seen on the back of the victim's door. There it was, the terrifying, ugly portrayal. Quickly, he picked up the rest of the charcoals and examined each one intently. The pesky thought was coming closer.

There was one portrait of a young boy with the words, "My Best Friend Tom" written underneath. A street scene, possibly a main street with shops lining each side, but no cars and no people. Another showed a school yard at recess time, all of the children jumping rope or chasing one another except for one lone little boy standing off by himself. Still another revealed a run-down wooden structure he recognized as the shed in the Fitch's back yard. A snake lay coiled in the sun outside the door of the shed.

As Beltz stared at the painting, he caught hold of the buzzing thought. The most important events or people in the artist's early life had been drawn in charcoal. The only one not drawn at that time was the crazy prophet. Of course, her nails. Verna must have used charcoal to draw that prophet just before she died.

He stood and quickly gathered up all the pictures and replaced them in the portfolio, keeping the prophet separate. This he placed in an empty folder he found on one of the shelves, tucked it under his arm and walked out of the room.

❧ TWENTY-TWO

"Lieutenant Beltz?"

"Yes."

"This is Janet Ross from the Ridgeleigh School in Boston. I'm returning your call of last week."

"Oh, thank you, Miss Ross. What have you got for me on Ellie Payne?"

"Well, she completed her freshman and sophomore years here. Our records indicate that Eleanor Payne was expelled very early in her junior year."

"Can you tell me why?" He could almost hear her eastern sniff at the other end.

"I suppose if this is serious—you say this is regarding a homicide?"

"Yes ma'am." Her voice was beginning to irritate him, high-pitched and condescending.

"So I can give you some details. I don't think that's out of order."

"I would appreciate some background."

"Well, it seems that even though she was young when she enrolled, there was already some emotional trauma in her past. When she was ten, her three year old sister drowned, practically in front of her eyes. She had taken the baby for a walk on the family's spacious grounds. The story went that Eleanor came screaming back to the house, telling her mother the baby had run ahead and fallen into the stream that ran through the property. The baby was dead by the time the mother reached her.

"When this occurred there was some question as to the veracity of the child's story, but the parents felt that by the time she came here, she had overcome any scandal or lingering guilt."

"How did the first two years go for her at Ridgeleigh?"

"Fine. There didn't seem to be any problem. She was very shy and didn't socialize much with the other girls. But she showed a distinct interest in the arts, particularly art history. I note here in the teacher's report that Eleanor might go into the teaching field. Of course, we can't keep up with all of our students."

"Of course."

"Now the episode regarding her dismissal. She lived in the junior dormitory in a three-bed room. There were four other bedrooms on that floor. One night Eleanor decided she would personally restyle the hair of some of her peers. At two a.m., with scissors in hand, she went from room to room, chopping willy-nilly at their long hair. And no doubt you know how important a girl's hair is at that age. She got to six girls before one of them awakened and screamed. An interesting foot-note here, Lieutenant Beltz. Her only victims were blondes. She left two brunettes and a red-head intact."

"Did Ellie...Eleanor ever explain why she did that?"

"Strangely no," she said, sniffing audibly this time.

"And that's why she was expelled? Was she prosecuted?"

"No. Her age precluded that. And her parents agreed to psychiatric therapy."

"Would you happen to know the doctor's name?" Beltz asked.

"Yes, but that is all I am prepared to tell you."

"Fine."

While writing down the doctor's name, Beltz thought that Plain Jane Ellie had some colorful past.

"Dr. Kiptide here. This is the earliest I could get back to you, Lieutenant Beltz. My patients come first, you know."

"I'm glad to hear that," Beltz said.

"The information you wanted about an Ellie Markham, who at the time she was my patient was Eleanor Payne, is privileged information, and of course I cannot divulge that to you."

"I appreciate that, Dr. Kiptide, but you do understand I am investigating a homicide. And Ellie did know the victim."

"That is unfortunate."

Another sniffer, Beltz thought. "How long was she in treatment?"

"A year and a half."

"Can you tell me her problem?"

"I cannot."

"At least can you tell me if she was cured of that problem?"

"That is something no one can tell you. A therapist can only show a patient the way and help her cope."

For Christ's sake, Beltz muttered to himself. They must take a course in psycho-babble before they can hang up that damn shingle.

"It would seem your patient had an antipathy for blondes. Can you tell me that much?"

"No. But what I can tell you Lieutenant, because it was in the police file and therefore public knowledge, is that her baby sister who drowned was a blonde. I hope that helps your investigation. But I really can't say anymore."

Beltz smiled. "Thank you Dr. Kiptide. I know your patients are waiting."

"If you're here to see my husband, he's not home, Lieutenant Beltz."

"No, I'd really like to talk to you, Mrs. Markham, if you can spare me the time."

"I was just preparing dinner. If you don't mind sitting in the kitchen we can talk."

"I like kitchens. They smell good. Let me guess. Pot roast?"

"Close. It's braciole." Ellie pulled out a chair at the kitchen table. "Here, sit. Can I get you a drink?"

"No, no, I'll just kibbitz." He sat and watched as she prepared a salad. "You know, Mrs. Markham, you're in the unique position of being acquainted with the victim before he had his surgery. Could you tell me what he was like? Would you say he was effeminate then? Mannerisms? Speech?"

"Not at all. I would say his movements were perfectly normal for a man. His voice was masculine. I never would have dreamed he yearned to be a female. But you must realize ours was just a surface relationship."

Beltz watched her chop onions and cucumbers on the butcher block built into the counter, then adroitly slide the pieces with the edge of the knife into the walnut salad bowl. "I'm surprised," he said, "that you don't have a food processor."

"Oh, I've been doing it this way for so long, I wouldn't know how to use one of those fancy gizmos." She began tearing at the head of lettuce.

"You said a surface relationship. Did he ever talk about anything except his art with you?"

"What do you mean?"

"His friends, family, perhaps a hobby.?"

Ellie appeared deep in thought. "Not that I recall. He was a devoted artist. You could tell that from his work. And so excited when we signed him up. Like a child who had just been given a pass to every ride in Disneyland."

Ellie smiled, reminiscing, the salad forgotten for the

moment. "I wish you could have seen him, Lieutenant, so thrilled putting his name at the bottom of that contract. Fortunately, he signed with us. Another agent might have taken advantage of his naiveté in the field."

She sliced a sliver of green pepper, then held the rest at one end and slowly munched on it until it was gone.

"Good veggies," she said. "Would you like some?"

"Thank you." He reached over the counter and helped himself to a radish. "I used to grow these when I had my own garden."

"He was a gentle boy," Ellie continued, ignoring Beltz, "gentle and kind and sweet. But nothing sexual about this boy at all. That's why the transformation came as such a shock. And you know, I never gave it a thought, that he sent his paintings by messenger. I knew he lived in town but all artists are a bit eccentric. Of course, now its obvious why."

"He had blond hair, right?"

"Yes, sort of shaggy, like a lot of the young men wear it. But neat."

Ellie began chopping faster on a plump, red tomato. "When I think," she said, her expression darkening, "that my husband slept with..."

"Don't dwell on that," Beltz said soothingly. "It's done with"

She finished the salad and placed the bowl in the refrigerator. When she began to set the table, he stood up.

"Well, I better be going." He walked slowly toward the front door. "Oh, Mrs. Markham, by the way, you don't like blondes very much, do you?"

The little color she had in her face drained. "What are you saying?"

"You know very well what I'm saying. Ridgeleigh School— 1967. Six blonde bobs all in a row?"

"How dare you dredge up something that happened when I was a sick and foolish child," she cried, furious. "What could that possibly have to do with this murder?"

He opened the door and turned slowly toward her. "I don't know, Mrs. Markham. But I aim to find out."

❧ TWENTY-THREE

Molly accepted eagerly when Stanley Beltz asked her to spend Wednesday, his day off, with him. She was waiting in the open doorway to the large red brick Georgian house at the end of the wooded lane.

When he drove up and said hello, he added, surprised, "I've never seen this part of Evanston. It's amazing; not like a city at all."

He walked around the front yard, admiring the roses and fall mums blooming vigorously alongside the south end. The tall evergreens on either side shielded the property from the houses next door. He was struck by the quiet, broken only by the chattering of the birds taking a bath.

He laughed out loud. "That's the funniest bird-bath I've ever seen."

"Not funny ha-ha," she protested, "maybe funny peculiar. It used to be a horse trough."

"With all that lacy grillwork?"

"Oh, that was the bottom of a Singer sewing machine. I soldered it on, myself."

"Mrs. Fast, you are a woman of many talents. You take

pictures for magazines and raise flowers and work with iron. This must be a great place for creative art, the peace and solitude."

"Would you like to come inside," she said, leading him up the front steps.

When she offered to show him the rest of the house, he followed her through room after room, up the stairs and down,his quick eye taking in the seemingly haphazard selection of furniture, lush plants, and the wonderful nooks and crannies not found in new homes. He marveled at pedestals with statues and shelves fairly bursting with wooden figures and mementos from years of travel. Each room was a mini library with books of every size and subject. The stairway wall was covered with large photographs: succulent fruits and vegetables dripping with moisture and a bevy of bathing beauties, none over three years old. There was also a portrait in black and white of a very handsome man. He did not ask who it was.

Her studio on the third floor gave him the most complete sense of Molly, not as a housewife, but as an artist. The room was all windows, with wooden boxes, each the size of a child's toy box along one wall. She opened each one and showed him her cameras, this one for close-ups, that one for portraits, another for long shots or landscapes. There were easels and flash equipment and strobe lights on bars, and lens caps all tucked neatly into their cloth bags.

"How long have you been at this?" Beltz asked.

"Forever, or it seems like that. I should be burned out by now, but I'm not. I'm one of those people who love to go to work."

"Well, it is right upstairs," he said, tweaking her.

"I know I'm lucky that way. But most of what I do is done someplace else. Finding props, schlepping them to the shoot, consults with clients...I can't do any of that here."

"And your darkroom?"

"Behind that door. I like to do my own developing. I'm

impatient. This way I can see my shots right away. Saves time."

When they were in his car driving north, Molly reminded him of his comment earlier, saying, "My part of Evanston is very old. That's why the houses are so large. Some of them even have servant's quarters or coach houses in the back."

When Beltz was surprised Molly did her own housework, she explained, "By the time I tell somebody what to clean or how I like it done, I can do it myself. Besides, I rarely do what's expected of me. Makes life more fun."

He drove slowly through the Winnetka ravine road and turned to smile at her. "You betcha."

"I've always been like that. Even as a kid. I had to do things my way."

"Tell me about it," he mumbled.

"When I was little, I had this habit of walking along the aisles of the five and ten, running my hand across the goodies I could barely see, and sometimes picking something up and pocketing it."

"You were never caught?"

"Oh I was caught all right." She laughed. "One bright spring day I decided I couldn't live without blue nail polish. I didn't realize they had changed the display. Where nail polish used to be, they now stocked the hardware, and little Molly pranced along, feeling for the bottle, and suddenly saw stars! I was too little to see the display—they had set a mousetrap with cheese. It caught my middle finger. Snap! I must have jumped two feet into the air. My crime spree ended right there." She thought for a moment, then said, "I bet you were a good little boy."

"Why? Because I'm a cop?"

"You impress me as a guy who always does the right thing at the right time."

"You make me sound boring," Beltz fretted.

But he didn't look boring. In fact, he thought he looked spiffy. He had taken great care this morning, choosing his camel sportcoat and gray flannel slacks with the gray sleeve-less sweater. The shirt was navy and gray plaid, button down, and the loafers were freshly shined. Maybe it was the day off after a particularly grinding week, or maybe it was this lady with the snapping blue eyes and the ready laugh. Whatever the reason, he felt like a man today, not a cop. Molly looked fetching in a pink hand-knit sweater and long plum skirt. She listened carefully, her animated face reflecting a spectrum of expression during their exchange. She no longer wore the rose.

Beltz parked in front of the Country Barn restaurant. When he began fishing in his pockets for change, Molly said, "Don't need it. Parking's free on Wednesdays."

"Of course," he mumbled, "that's how the rich get richer."

They sat on the enclosed terrace and each ordered the poached salmon and a California Riesling. Beltz was hungry. Breakfast had been a cup of instant coffee and dry toast, and when the basket of hot rolls and blueberry muffins came, he spread on the sweet butter and shook his head appreciatively.

"Time was, you know, when sweet butter was found only in Kosher restaurants," he said to Molly, "but now it's served in the finest places."

"It's probably bad for you," she said, grimacing, "everything good is bad for you nowadays."

"Not you, too?" he said with a groan, remembering Ziv Goldberg's advice. They enjoyed the tender salmon flavored with a delicate dill sauce, and the exquisitely dry wine. The terrace was less crowded than the main room, their small talk thus easy and unforced. Neither brought up the homicide. Just before leaving, he saw Molly pop the last blueberry muffin into her purse, and chided her as they walked outside.

"I thought you gave up thieving."

"It's for later. I always get hungry around four." She laughed. "It's a habit."

"Like snooping, huh?"

When they reached Lake Forest, Beltz parked, and they walked around Market Square. Shops lined the little park on both sides, built to simulate the outbuildings of a castle or palace. The style was tudor, with dark wood and heavy stone walls; old money, he thought. Nothing ostentatious here.

"It's a different world," he said, taking her arm as they strolled. "Here, one wouldn't know the dirt and crime of the city existed."

"That's not so bad, but the city has life and art, and stimulation. You can't get that here."

Molly stopped in front of one of the shop windows featuring frilly lingerie. "I don't care what they say, Stanley, a man who's been changed surgically into a woman is still a man inside."

"This is my day off, remember?"

"But it's fascinating. And I've been reading about it. Do you think Verna was a prostitute?"

"I don't think so," he said thoughtfully, "at least not in the usual sense."

Molly pursed her lips, thought a moment, then took a deep breath and spoke her next sentence like a memorized recitation.

"The experts say that the male to female transsexual needs constant reinforcement of her new femininity, and that if she doesn't marry, she might turn to prostitution. It makes sense. They can't change their chromosomes, you know."

Beltz smiled. "You *have* been reading. That bit about chromosomes is true if you base their gender on XY or XX. Otherwise, it's all in their heads."

Molly pondered his statement as she studied the ruffled nightgown in the window. "Stanley, I'm so curious. How could they be fooled? The men she slept with, I mean."

"I guess I've read the same books you have, Molly, and I still can't believe it. It must be one hell of a surgery."

They crossed the square to the ice cream parlor and

ordered two giant scoops of chocolate jamoca fudge, and continued their stroll along Western Avenue, licking at their cones.

"Just how I like it," Beltz said, "nice and hard. I'm one of those strange people who like hard ice cream and overcooked meat. Comes from my mother's idea that if she cooked kosher meat long enough, it would be tender. It never was. It tasted like the bottom of a shoe."

"My parents traveled a lot so I guess I read so much because I was lonely."

"What kind of books did you read?"

"Mostly Nancy Drew mysteries, but I finally moved on to Sherlock Holmes and Agatha Christie."

"Ah-hah! That's how it started."

"The game's afoot!" She laughed. "It was so much fun trying to figure them out. But I was always wrong."

"Me, I liked Mark Twain and Dickens."

"Stanley?"

"Molly?"

"About Verna...what causes this to happen in some people? I've heard the mother has something to do with it. And I've heard that the father has something to do with it."

"It could be one or the other, or both, or neither. That doesn't say much for our psychiatric community, does it?"

"Well," she challenged, "how can they go ahead and operate in all these hospitals...I think it's something like thirty around the country...without knowing more about the cause?"

"Let me tell you, it's a helluva lot safer than running off to a dirty room somewhere in Casablanca. That's where they used to go."

"Bummer!"

"Mm-mm." Beltz leaned down and kissed away the drop of chocolate near her mouth. It wasn't a romantic gesture, yet it made him feel very young and gallant. And the scent of her perfume left him light-headed for a moment.

Molly was touched by his unexpected tenderness, and she felt a sudden glow of pleasure in the shared moment. Then she shivered and took his arm. "Let's go into the hotel and warm up for a while."

The Woodland Inn had a cozy fire going in the fireplace of the pseudo English drawing room. A game table nearby held a scrabble set.

"Come over here, lady, and let's pit my City College against your Northwestern lit. And no two-letter words allowed."

Molly grew impatient with Beltz's lengthy deliberations and fidgeted restlessly, finally pulling a piece of paper from her skirt pocket.

"Listen to this, Stanley. I copied it out of a library book. 'Typically, the mother keeps the male infant to herself. She gratifies his wishes instantly, whenever possible. She enjoys and encourages actions which keep the child close to her and discourages attempts to move away.'"

"Molly, enough already."

"No, let me finish."

He sighed and studied the board.

"'However, as the child grows,'" Molly continued, "'the mother may not be able to handle aggressive and active play, and directs the male child to quieter activities and to quieter companions, possibly girls. Gradually, the child learns that feminine actions bring a positive response from the mother and other members of the family.' And," Molly went on, almost without pausing for breath, "the book also discusses the absent father syndrome...either real..."

"You mean, in fact or by effect, right?" Beltz said, without looking up.

"Yes. Exactly!"

"Look. I've got a fifty!" Beltz put every tile from his rack on the triple word score, adding the word QUARTER to the word BACK already on the board. "How's that? I get seventy-five. Give up?"

"I will if you answer my question."

"Okay. What's on your mind?"

"This paragraph I just read. You've met the parents. Are they like that?"

Beltz sat back in his chair. "It's difficult to say. May Fitch is rather a stern, humorless person, unhappy, perhaps,with her lot in life. I can't imagine her ever smiling. She reminds me of the way the early American settlers were drawn, drab and overworked. Unloved," he added softly. He turned and saw her watching him, concentrating on every word.

"And the father?" Molly asked.

"A big man physically, huge shoulders, large hands. Doesn't talk much. Insignificant, I'd say."

"Then they fit the pattern, don't you see?"

"I've thought of that."

Molly began dismantling the game, placing the tiles and racks in the box. "Poor kid," she said, "his parents must have thought he was a real freak."

"Freak? You want to know about freaks? Let me tell you, Molly," Beltz admonished. "When I was a kid, my dad took me to a state fair. I begged him to take me into the freak tent. When we got inside, this tall...person, dressed in a flowing gown, stood on the stage. It looked like a woman, but talked in a very deep voice.

"It had huge breasts. It told us about being married three times, twice to a woman, once to a man. Now remember, I was a kid, the age when lectures are ignored or forgotten entirely. But I remember every word of this one.

"Anyway, the person raised that long skirt. The body was naked underneath, and I saw huge hairy legs and a thick bush of black pubic hair. Suddenly, it spread its thighs and reached down and pulled out a long, normal penis from within the vagina. I hid my face against my father's sleeve.

"I had bad dreams for weeks afterwards. These are the freaks that need this surgery. Maybe science is taking it too far."

They sat in silence. After a while, Beltz stood and stretched. "I'm ready for a drink. They have a dining room here?"

"Yes, a lovely one. And in spite of that disgusting story you just told me, I'm hungry."

Walking Molly to her front door later that evening, Beltz told her how much he enjoyed the day, how he hadn't taken a day off since his wife died. He hoped they could be together again soon.

She said, "What about right now?"

The next morning, Beltz bounded down her front steps, realizing he hadn't felt this good since stealing a kiss from Alice Greenebaum in the back seat of her father's Studebaker the night of the junior prom.

❧ TWENTY-FOUR

On Thursday morning, Governor Rupert was meeting with his Fine Arts Committee. One of his advisors on the board recommended that he really ought to include a young Illinois artist among those displayed on the office walls. It might not be a bad idea, he went on, to inaugurate an artist-of-the-month contest, and honor the recipient at his monthly news conference.

The governor agreed, and knowing the Markhams from a previous purchase, called their gallery after the committee meeting, and asked them to bring him some work done by Illinois artists. He would make the choices himself. He didn't need a committee.

When Ellie hung up the phone, Bob asked, "Who was it?"

"The governor."

"What governor?"

"Of Illinois."

"Governor Rupert?"

"Is there another governor of Illinois?"

"Well…what did he say?"

"He wants me to bring over some paintings."

"He just bought three a couple of months ago," Bob said.

"These would be for his offices in Chicago."

"He must have told you what he was interested in."

"He did."

"What are we playing? Twenty questions? We're still running a business, aren't we?"

"When you're not off doing other things."

"Okay, Ellie, knock it off."

"Au contraire, hubby dear, that's your department."

"Jesus, Ellie, what do you want from me. I've apologized. You want more? You want me to grovel?"

"No. I want you to tell me how sick you must feel every time you think about screwing a man with a cunt!"

Bob whirled on her, his hand outstretched. But he didn't strike her. Something held him back.

"Go ahead. Hit me. Does that give you a hard-on? Maybe that's one way you get your kicks."

"Stop it, Ellie," he said between clenched teeth. "You want out? You can have out."

Her sarcastic smile vanished. "What else can I have?"

"Not a goddam thing. It's all mine. You brought nothing to it. You'll take nothing away."

"Are you forgetting it was my knowledge and my skill in signing young artists that brought the gallery its success? Without me, you never would have made it. Your money would have gone right down the sewer, where you are, now."

"Shut your mouth, Ellie."

She turned and walked to the window, stiff-backed and dry-eyed. "It's going to snow."

There was a long chilly silence. "Now what shall we get together to bring the governor?" Bob asked. "He wants only Illinois artists?"

Tersely, she answered, "Something about an artist-of-the-month award."

"Nice. It's about time." He moved toward the gallery. "I'll get them together."

"Oh no you won't," she shouted, "I'm going to do it and I'm going to take them there."

He turned. "Let me tell you this, Ellie. If you put your bitchiness aside to help me make selections, then we can work together. If not, I'll do it alone."

She stared at him. Where had he found his balls all of a sudden? "All right! He wants us there by two."

The new State of Illinois building had been a bone in the taxpayers' craw since the design was first made public. The building faced south, and the solid wall of glass trapped the sun's heat, the temperature in the interior offices soaring to over ninety-eight degrees during its first summer. Television news stories poked fun at it, newspaper editorials screamed WASTE! WASTE! and Governor Rupert, who had rammed the funding bill through the state legislature, was dubbed the governor with the edifice complex.

The governor's offices were on the sixteenth floor, a rambling warren of connecting suites furnished with valuable antiques. His opponents often denounced him for the time spent collecting rather than tending to business.

The building rose like a glass rhombus from the heart of the loop, that area of downtown Chicago surrounded by the elevated trains. After that first summer, the engineers improved the air-conditioning somewhat. Winters were less of a problem. Except during heavy snowfalls, when funneling winds pasted the blowing snow to the glass walls. No one could see out. It was like working in an igloo.

At two o'clock the building was teeming with people: office workers and pages poured in and out of elevators, and lawyers, clients and patrons packed the lower level restaurant. The huge atrium was the focus of the structure, reaching from the lower level to the very top of the glass roof and taking up the bulk of square footage. Each floor had its own walkway around the half-circle, with low railings considered by some to be dangerous and unequal to the task of protecting anyone looking down.

Bus tours were lining up outside waiting to disgorge their passengers into the grand entrance. Bob and Ellie's taxi had to pull up to a side door, the driver grumbling because of the one-way streets and the snarled mid-afternoon traffic.

They unloaded six canvases and struggled into the elevator along with the crowd. When they reached the sixteenth floor, they carefully edged their way out and walked halfway around the walkway to the governor's office.

His assistant greeted them, ushered them into the governor's suite, brought them coffee, and said Governor Rupert would be with them shortly.

Bob and Ellie unwrapped the paintings and stood them against the wall. A short biography of each artist was taped to the back of the canvases.

"Good to see you both again," Governor Rupert said as he entered the room. A big florid man looking tan and robust despite the time of year, the governor's handshake was solid and a bit too hard. As if saying, here I am, in complete control.

He studied the paintings. "Ah! These are very good. This might be a difficult choice. Perhaps you could advise me."

"If you wish, Governor," Bob said nervously.

Ellie spoke up. "I personally think that Hammerman landscape is the best, and he shows the most promise. We've sold several of his. And he was born and raised in Pekin, Illinois."

Ellie paused only long enough to dab at the perspiration on her upper lip. "Unless you want a black." She posed with a hand on her hip. "Then I would choose this Ellison. She's out of the projects. It would be good P.R. And she's talented. You can just feel her hunger."

Bob was furious with Ellie's heavy-handed takeover. He tried to break in. "Now wait a minute…"

"No, no," Governor Rupert interrupted. "I agree with her. That Ellison is good. Probably the best of the lot here. And a black—that's a good idea. I like it. Would you mind leaving them here for a few days? I'd like my wife to take a look."

"Of course," they said, almost in unison.

"I'll get back to you." The governor walked them to the door. "Thanks again. You're a good team." His head kept nodding as if he were agreeing with himself.

They walked out through the suites to the walkway. Throngs of people pushed and shoved, hoping to get a glance at the governor. Ellie and Bob were in the middle of the press of humanity moving towards the elevators. Before they knew it, they were against the railing overlooking the wide expansive atrium.

Suddenly a sickening scream rang out from the restaurant down in the lower level. Then others, infected by the hysteria, joined in the shrill and soaring cry, until the atrium echoed with the agony of the plunge.

⚘ TWENTY-FIVE

Lieutenant Stanley Beltz returned to a day's worth of desk work on Thursday morning. He had uncompleted reports to finish and telephone calls to make about more than one case. But the pile of papers on his desk was ridiculous.

"Who's been sitting at my desk?" he bellowed.

"Not me, Papa Bear," three cops answered in unison.

"Come on, come on, whose crap is this?" Beltz peered closely at the top sheet. "Who's got the shoplifter at the Lincoln Mall?" He sailed the paper over their heads. "Who's collar is the pickpocket on Armitage?" Another sheet soared, landing at Brankowsky's feet.

"Cut it out, Lieutenant, I had to use your desk yesterday. That's my stuff," Brankowsky admitted.

"You had a busy day. You'd think with the cold weather, the goons would all stay home."

"Naw," Jake said, "the holiday season is upon us and they're working on their shopping lists."

"Take this pile." Beltz handed the papers to Jake. "I need the space. One lousy day off and I'm backed up again."

"Have fun?" Jake asked.

"Yep."

"Gonna tell me about it?"

"Nope."

"Well, at least we're the beneficiaries of your smiling face and sweet disposition this morning." Jake snapped his cap on his head and walked out of the station.

Beltz was already on the phone to the Indian Center. He knew the Chief was working at the moving company and this would be a good time to talk to the administrator.

The lieutenant had known Johnny Fox since the lawyer had taken on the job at the Center ten years ago. At first, Fox worked as a public defender, mostly with his own people. He was glib, with an extensive vocabulary and a flair for the dramatic; many times his clever spiels in court moved juries in his favor. The State's Attorney's office always sent their best assistants to oppose him in court, but they lost more cases than they won.

But Fox felt a strong obligation to the adolescent Indian boys in Uptown. Because he didn't want them going the way of the black or hispanic gangs, when United Charities opened the Indian Center on Wilson Avenue, Fox agreed to be its administrator. He continued to conduct his law practice from the small office in the Center with three phones and his secretary Patsy, who juggled both his careers.

"Hi, Patsy. Stanley Beltz here. Your boss around?"

"Lieutenant, where have you been?"

"Busy."

"Too busy to come to the Center and see your friends? Shame."

"You're right. I'll get there soon. Where's the good counselor?"

"I'll get him. Hold on."

Beltz hated to be put on hold, but he hated the rotten music some people played during the wait even more. He was glad this wasn't one of them.

"Hi, Stash! Oy, have I missed you. How you was?"

"Hey, Johnny, many moons have passed since we had big pow-wow."

"Hoo-ha! A real Indian maven."

Beltz laughed. "It's been a long time. Anyway, tell me, have you been satisfied with George Burning Tree? You know, working with the boys and all. He a good leader? Patient with the kids?"

"What's this about, Stash?" Fox was suddenly the attorney, alert and on guard. "He in some kind of trouble?"

"I'm not sure. He *is* out on bail right now, you know, for beating up that reporter. But I think the charges will be dropped."

"Yeah, I heard about that. But no problem here. He shows up all the time. The kids like him. He's done a lot for our boys in the area. A good role model. Doesn't drink. Doesn't throw his weight around. And the kids are really looking forward to his workshop starting up again for the holidays."

"What kind of workshop?"

"A wood carving class. You didn't know about those beautiful little animals he carves for the gift shop? They're Christmas decorations. Make a lot of money for us too. He does it every year."

"Good with the knife, huh?"

There was silence on the other end of the line. Then Fox said, "Hey, wait a minute, where's this leading? You think he's involved in that girl's murder?"

"I don't know."

"You pull him in, I'm right there behind him, Stash."

"I would expect you to be."

"Is he a suspect?"

"Yes."

"Big suspect? Little suspect? So-so?"

"Mm-mm, so-so. If it was any better than that, you'd know about it."

"I'm counting on that."

"When are these workshops?"

"Why? You wanna learn to carve animals?"

"Maybe."

"Or you wanna see how a Sioux Indian handles a knife?"

"Don't cross-examine me yet, Johnny. It might not get that far."

"Okay. Friday nights at eight. Saturday at one. Schmuck! Maybe you'll be busy both times. If I have any mazel, that is."

"Thanks Johnny. You heap big friend."

Beltz spent the next three hours completing his reports and cleaning up the paper work. He hated paper work. He felt he was drowning in paper work. If the public only knew that a detective spent more time on paper work than on detecting, they wouldn't think it's such a romantic job. He'd gladly give a years' supply of egg bagels if he could have a little person sitting on his desk doing all his paper work for him.

He stood, stretched, and realized how hungry he was. The clock on the wall said three. He'd give Molly a call, and then go out for lunch.

He dialed her number. "Hello…"

"Molly? I just called…"

"…home right now, but if you'll leave a message, I'll get back to you. If I feel like it. If I don't, you won't hear from me."

He hung up. At least her tape was a little different than most. He had to smile. A pure original, but great in bed. He blushed, looked around to see if anyone had been watching, and wrote a memo to himself to call her later.

It was much colder today, one of those raw damp days with a leaden sky. The clouds were heavy and restless, eager to dump their stuffing of snow on the city below. He pulled up his coat collar, jammed his hands in his pockets, and realized he'd left his beeper on his desk. But lunch won't take long. He hurried along the two blocks to Mandel's Deli on the corner of Hoyne and Belmont. This would be the day for his good fat corned beef sandwich and bowl of barley soup he allowed himself once a week.

163

He wondered how long Mandel's could last in this neighborhood. The graffiti had changed over the years, from the Appalachian Dukes to the Tribal Warriors, to the Latin Saints. There were orientals living here too, and East Indians, but they weren't as artistically inclined as the others. The newest brightest paint belonged to the Black Dudes. They always moved in last. Somebody had to be on the bottom.

"Hell-ooo, Stanley!" Morry Mandel sang out from behind the counter. "How's the crime business?"

Beltz always enjoyed seeing Morry. He never changed. The same broad smile, the same rotund belly beneath the stained apron. He was bald and swarthy, the black eyes darting everywhere. Beltz had been kidding him for years about his fat corned beef. But that was the only way he really liked it.

"It's good, unfortunately," Beltz answered. "The bad guys never sleep."

"Good soup today, or do you want the barley?"

"Make me an offer."

"Matzo ball? Black bean?"

"Give me the barley. And a mile-high fat corned beef." He stressed the word FAT.

"I've got another kind?" Morry asked. "I suppose you want a pickle too?"

"What's corned beef without a pickle?"

As he ate, the store filled with customers, and from the chalk board menu, Beltz could see that Morry was moving with the times. Tacos and burritos, egg rolls and fried rice, and collard greens and black-eyed peas had been added to the gefilte fish and kreplach. From a little corner deli, it was developing into a regular bazaar of international cuisine. He laughed to himself. Mandel's would last longer than he had thought.

He finished eating and went to the register to pay his bill.

"How's the murder case coming along?" Mandel asked, giving Beltz his change. "That was some shocker, huh?" He bent closer to the detective. There were people nearby.

"That girl, she was a man? What kind of *mishegoss* is that? Did you see it?"

"Yeah."

"You mean...his *schvantz* was gone? Oy!" He shook his head.

"Gone, Morry, gone. What's a *mishegoss* to us is a *mechiah* to someone else. Don't even try to understand it."

"You see all kinds, don't you?"

"Yep." Beltz smiled. "But judging from your menu, so do you."

"Listen, you gotta go with the flow. Am I hep or am I hep?"

"You're hep. So long, Morry."

At five minutes after four, headquarters was crawling with cops, reporters, television cameras and wires stretching across desks and chairs. Floodlights were coming on and somebody was bellowing instructions. Walking in, Beltz thought it looked like a goddamn movie set.

"Stan, for Christ's sake, I thought you'd never get back." Captain Weigel rushed him into his office.

"What the hell's going on here?" Beltz demanded.

"We've either got a jumper or a homicide on our hands."

"Who?"

"Markham. One of your murder suspects, I think."

"Which one? Bob? Or Ellie?"

"Bob. Went over the railing at the State of Illinois building about an hour ago."

"Jesus! What...?"

"That's all I know," the captain said, sitting behind his desk. "They called us. The uniform called First District Headquarters...they knew it was your case. You're to get in touch with..." He consulted the message slip on his desk. "...Detective Menoni. Here's the number. Bum break, huh?"

Beltz took the paper and walked to his desk. It was bathed

165

in light. Floods were aimed at him, and reporters were shouting questions before he even sat down.

"Lieutenant Beltz, what does this do to your murder case?"

"Hey, Lieutenant, do you think he was guilty?"

"Was he pushed? Was it murder?"

"Could it have been an accident?"

Beltz put both hands out. "Wait a minute! One at a time! And I'm not going to have all these answers for you now."

"Have a heart, Beltz. Give us something. People want to know."

"I don't care about your five o'clock news or your morning deadline. This is a murder case. You'll know when I know."

"Was Markham a suspect? Does this screw up your case?"

Beltz whirled on the reporter. "Where'd you get that?"

"Hell, Menoni..."

"Oh, swell!"

A reporter in the rear hollered, "What about his wife?"

Beltz turned his back.

"Is she involved?"

"No comment."

One of the anchor men from Channel 2, a feisty little guy who dug up facts on his own mostly to embarrass the crooked aldermen, moved to the front of the crowd. Beltz always liked him. Somebody had to dig out all the dirty facts and shake up the voters.

He said to Beltz, "Sir, if we came back in a few hours for the ten o'clock news, would you be able to give us any details?"

"I don't know. Call me first. Right now, everybody out!"

❧ TWENTY-SIX

Bob Markham's body was taken to the Cook County Morgue, while Ellie, in shock, was transported by ambulance to Lake Shore Memorial Hospital. She had been hysterical and incoherent, and the uniformed patrolman first on the scene felt she needed immediate medical attention. Her protests were ignored. She kicked at the ambulance attendants and swore at the doctors in the emergency room.

It was close to six o'clock when Lieutenant Beltz reached the fourth floor nurses' station and asked to see Ellie Markham. The nurse was hesitant. The attending doctor had warned her to admit only members of the patient's family. No reporters. She assumed he also meant police. She'd better check.

Dr. Bergman was a short nervous man with spikey black hair. He looked like he'd plugged himself into an electrical socket. Not only was every hair on edge, his whole body was in constant motion, hands gesturing, feet shifting weight, fingers tapping on the desk top. He spoke hurriedly to Beltz, constantly readjusting his glasses. It made Beltz jumpy just to watch him.

"She's under sedation, so don't ask her too many questions. And don't stay too long."

Beltz asked, "Does she realize what happened?"

"I'm sure she must know her husband is dead, but I don't think she's aware of how it took place."

"Did she say anything to you when she was brought in?"

Bergman smirked, picking up the tempo of his finger-tapping. "She said plenty, four-letter words I never even heard of. And I thought I knew them all."

"No," Beltz said, "I meant about the husband's fall."

"She kept going on and on about how bad she felt...how it was an accident...how it wasn't her fault."

Beltz frowned. "Anything else?"

"No. After a while she wasn't very lucid."

"Where's her room?"

"Down that hall, Room 402. And remember, don't stay long."

Poor guy, Beltz thought, he needs a sedative himself.

He knocked first, then opened the door to Ellie's room. She was turned away from him, lying on her side facing the window.

"Mrs. Markham? Are you awake?" he said softly.

"Hmm?" She turned slowly in the bed and Beltz was shocked at the sight of her haggard face.

"It's Lieutenant Beltz, Mrs. Markham. May I come in?"

She said nothing and he walked closer to the bed. "I'm awfully sorry about what happened."

"What happened?"

"Don't you remember, Mrs. Markham?"

"You mean about the baby?"

"Tell me about the baby," Beltz said kindly, wondering if there was any sense in questioning her further. She seemed to be somewhere else.

"We were holding hands...she broke away...I ran after her...the trees were in the way. I screamed...no one heard me...I kept calling her. Sharon! Sharon! Come back. The water...the water..."

Beltz watched her closely, fascinated by the performance. Her eyes were glassy, staring vacantly. They had no color. Her voice had risen two octaves when she shouted the child's name. Was it the sedative working on her memory, or had her mind snapped? In any case, reality had ceased to exist for Ellie Markham, and he wasn't going to learn about Bob's death-fall in this room.

He tip-toed out and closed the door.

In the hospital lobby, Beltz spied a public phone booth and decided to try calling Molly again. He cut off the message and hung up.

His car was parked on Superior Street in a No Parking zone, but the sign in the front window reading Officer On Duty usually did the trick. Unfortunately, the meter maid had not bothered to look in the window. He had a twenty-dollar ticket under the wiper. More paper work.

The security guard had only been on the job at the State of Illinois building for one month. His previous job had been night watchman for an all-night photo developing company, and the closest he had ever come to crowd control was watching the change of shifts at eleven each week night.

"I said this problem would come up one day. Somebody's gonna jump or fall...mark my words. I wish to hell I wasn't on duty when the first one did it."

The guard had been told to wait for Lieutenant Beltz at the lobby entrance at six forty-five. He was a solemn, long-faced man with a large nose and horsy yellow teeth. His uniform shirt was stained with sweat across the back and under the arms, and the pants were flash-flood style, hemmed far too short of his black crepe soled shoes.

Still upset by the horrendous incident of the afternoon, his stained fingers shook as he chain-smoked, and he protested all the while that he had warned the building manager about the railings. They were much too low to be safe.

"Exactly where were you when this occurred?" Beltz asked him.

"In front of the governor's offices."

"How far was that from the actual spot where he fell?"

"Oh, about eighteen or twenty feet."

"Would you show me?"

They took the elevator up to the top floor. A yellow police ribbon barred the walkway on each side of the governor's office. The guard moved these aside to show Beltz the precise spot where he had been standing.

"I was right here, right next to the entrance. And all these people were in front of me. Christ, I don't know where they all come from. Looking this way and that trying to see the governor. Like he was a damn movie star, or something. Busiest day we've had since I've been here."

"Did you see anything at all?"

"Hell, I couldn't see a thing. This place was jammed." He lit another cigarette. "I hear the guy who was killed had just been in seeing the governor. Is that right?"

"Yes, that's right. Did you see them when they first came in? He was with his wife."

"Nope. Guess I was on my break then."

"How long is your break?"

"About fifteen minutes. I guess I left around two. So I must have missed them coming in."

"Did you see them coming out?"

"I might have. But lots of people go in and out of here."

"So tell me, how did you know when it happened?"

"I heard these terrible screams, and all this commotion going on up here."

"Screams?"

"Yep. First from up here and then from down below. When the body must have hit."

"What did you do first?"

"I made everybody get back and stand against the wall."

He flattened himself against the blue glass panels, illustrating the order he had given. "This one lady wouldn't move. Just stood there looking down. Like she was in a trance or something. I got scared. I thought, listen! She could take a jump too!"

"What makes you say jump?"

"Well, jump, got pushed, who knows? With so many people and..."

"Any of the governor's staff say they saw anything?"

"Wouldn't your officers know that?" the guard asked, grinding his cigarette out with his heel on the polished floor.

"Well, I thought you might have heard some talk around the office here."

"No, I didn't hear any."

"You're sure now, you've told me everything? Even if there's something you think unimportant..."

The guard thought hard, his face all screwed up, then said, "Nope. I told you everything."

They went downstairs in the elevator and Beltz thanked him. He spoke briefly to the uniforms on duty, then left the building.

The night shift had begun by the time Beltz returned to headquarters. He checked his messages on the spindle; there was nothing except some reporters wanting interviews. And one he could barely make out. Sergeant Neal's writing. It looked like a Mrs. East called. There was a question mark like Neal hadn't gotten the spelling right. She would call back later. Mrs. East? He called Neal at home.

"Listen Mike, this message here, with the question mark. Who called me? Mrs. somebody. Was it East?"

"No, that doesn't sound right."

"Was it Fast?"

"Yeah, yeah, that was it. I wasn't sure. That's why I put the question mark."

"Thanks, pal, and buy yourself a sharp pencil."

"Or a hearing aid. Ha-ha-ha."

Beltz hung up and called Molly. Still not home. Or not taking phone calls. Unlikely. Hadn't she said clients called at all hours?

He opened the Lake murder folder and looked up Dr. Kiptide's number. The answering service was adamant; they wouldn't give out his home number if Beltz was the King of England. But if he would leave his number, they would call the doctor and give him the message. If the doctor wished, he would call the detective back.

Beltz waited. Ten minutes later, his phone rang.

"Lieutenant Beltz? You have more questions?"

"Not so much a question, Doctor, as much as an educated opinion."

"Fire ahead." The good doctor sounded like he'd already had his happy hour. Beltz wished he'd had his.

"About Mrs. Markham. Do you think a shocking event now could trigger a psychotic response?"

"It depends on what it is."

Beltz explained the incident at the State of Illinois building and Ellie's subsequent behavior.

There was a pause.

When the doctor came back on the line, he said, "How dreadful. Of course, if what you say is true, there is always the possibility that the patient could lose touch with all reality and revert to a previous traumatic experience. Now you realize I have not examined the patient. This is only a long-distance guess. And we would have to observe her over a period of time. But I doubt if questioning her further will bear much fruit. At least for the present. However, she could snap out of it tomorrow. You never know about the human mind."

"Could she be faking?"

"Hardly likely. I never thought she had that much imagination. Of course, she could have learned in the meantime."

"Hm-mm."

"I'm sorry, Lieutenant, that I can't be more helpful. Perhaps the doctors treating her can give you additional information. And tell them if they need any background, they can call me."

"Them you'll talk to?"

"Them I'll talk to."

The night desk sergeant poked his head around the door of Beltz's office. "Lieutenant, come out here and talk to these guys. They're hollering about their ten o'clock broadcast. Can't you give them some crumbs and get them out of my hair?"

There was nothing to tell the news people. But they waited like vultures in the outer reception area, ready to pick him clean.

"Listen, ladies and gentlemen, I wish I had something to report," he said to the group. "All I can tell you is that the investigation is on-going; the body of Mr. Markham is at the Cook County Morgue for autopsy. Mrs. Markham has been hospitalized but no, I said NO visitors allowed. We're treating the incident as a possible suicide, accident, or homicide."

The Channel 2 newsman asked, "Does this, in your opinion, tie in with the Verna Lake murder?"

"I can't tell you at this time."

A female reporter, wearing large horn-rimmed glasses and a brown felt fedora asked, "The Lake murder would be solved if Markham was your murderer, wouldn't it, Lieutenant Beltz?"

"I would say that assumption is premature, Miss...?"

"It's Ms. *Ms.* Shannon, Lieutenant. Liz Shannon."

"Fine."

Another reporter shoved a microphone in Beltz's face and annoyed, Beltz pushed the mike away. "That's it. I just told you Mrs. Markham is in deep shock. In the hospital. And if I hear about any one of you trying to see her, that one will be persona non grata in this station. And that means OUT!"

As he turned and walked away, a smart-ass voice rang out. "Hey, Beltz! Do you think both Markhams might have been screwing around with Verna? You know, her being both sexes?"

Without looking around, Beltz marched into his office and slammed the door.

He picked up the list of witnesses Detective Menoni had given him over the phone, and began calling them.

The first was a Mrs. Fanny Paperniak, visiting the building with a senior center from the north side. She had been standing with her tour group near the entrance to the governor's suite, but she had been so busy hanging on to her pocketbook, as their counselor had warned, that she hadn't seen a thing. But Mrs. Feldstein might be able to tell him more. See, she talked about it all the way back on the bus, that she thought he'd been pushed.

Beltz thanked her and hung up and checked his list. Mrs. Feldstein's number was third down. He dialed.

After identifying himself, he asked, "Can you tell me about the man who fell from the walkway this afternoon?"

"I sure can," Mrs. Feldstein said emphatically. "I saw the whole thing! He was pushed! I saw it."

"What did you see?"

"I was standing not more than two feet away…and there were a lot of people…pushing and shoving…they have no respect for age anymore. When I was a young…"

"Two feet away from where, Mrs. Feldstein?"

"Well, two feet away from the man…and the woman he was with."

"How do you know they were together?"

"They said on the news he was with his wife."

"Did you see her?"

"I…I think so. There was a woman standing next to him."

"Was there more than one woman standing next to him?"

"Well, sure, there were lots of women there."

"Did you actually see him fall?"

"I saw him when I looked over the railing."

"Mrs. Feldstein, did you actually see him go over the railing?"

"He was pushed."

Suddenly, Beltz heard the sound of the receiver dangling, bumping the wall. A minute later, another voice came on the line.

"Officer? This is Irene Gordon, Mrs. Feldstein's daughter. I want to explain to you that my mother is suffering from Alzheimer's Disease, and we just don't know when she's telling the truth or living in her dream world. I wouldn't put too much stock in what she told you. I'm sorry."

"I'm sorry too, Mrs. Gordon."

"I'm afraid this was her moment to be in the limelight, and nothing more."

After this conversation, Beltz could feel a zinger of a headache coming on. Maybe he should send out for a sandwich before calling more witnesses. First he'd try Molly.

It was after eight, and she was still not home. Where the hell was she? Maybe he was being foolish, but he was beginning to fret about her absence. Not knowing her schedule, there was nothing he could do, no one else to call. He'd try later.

The next three witnesses on the list were not at home, and the honeymoon couple at a downtown hotel claimed they saw nothing.

The priest visiting with his choir boys from Sheboygan, was terribly upset about the whole happening. But he had been too busy herding his noisy young charges to have paid attention. However, one of the lads claimed to have seen the man jump. He gave Beltz the boy's number, blessed him in his good work, and hung up.

Beltz spoke briefly with the boy's mother, then asked if he could talk to Dwayne.

"Yessir, this is Dwayne."

"Son, I know you've had a busy, tiring day, but if you

could tell me what you saw on the sixteenth floor of the State of Illinois building this afternoon, I would appreciate it."

"Okay. Like, it was real crowded up there, you know? And hot. And you could hardly stand, there were so many people. And I was trading baseball cards with a friend and out of the side of my eye I thought I saw this guy get up on the railing and then he jumped. I mean, like one second he was there, and then he was gone. You know?"

"I know how you must feel, Dwayne, it must have been terrible for you to see. But I want you to think back to the moment you were trading cards until you said the man jumped."

The boy caught his breath, as though dredging up the memory. Beltz could almost hear the gears shifting in reverse.

"Okay. I was trading Shawon Dunston for Cal Ripken. That's because, well, my friend wanted Mark Grace too, and I was looking at him trying to decide if Ripken was worth it, you know? And sort of sideways in my eye, I saw a person standing up above the crowd...and then when I looked, he was gone."

"Out of the side of your eye. Did you actually see the man standing on the railing? Or, let's say, Dwayne, could it have been a tall person who had come into your view?"

"No, sir, I saw this man."

"You're sure it was a man."

"Yes sir."

"It wasn't a woman wearing slacks?"

"Well, I saw a flash of blue. I remember it was blue, like jeans. And I turned my head, and that's when I saw him fall."

"Did you see anything else?"

"What do you mean?"

"Was anyone standing very close to him?"

"Lots of people."

The detective was silent, then said, "You've been real help-ful, Dwayne. Will you talk to me again if I call?"

"Sure."

"Thanks. And I hope you didn't trade Mark Grace."

"No way," the boy replied.

The last four witnesses on Beltz's list each had a story as convincing as young Dwayne's, only completely different. One said the man was wearing a brown suit, another claimed he yelled Down With Taxes before jumping, and still another said he was sure the crowd pushed him over accidentally, and the wife ought to sue.

The witnesses were running true to form. One of the first things he learned in the academy was the unreliability of eye witnesses all too eager to do their civic duty. In something as simple as a two-car accident, there could be as many versions as the number of bystanders who saw it.

He dialed Molly again, heard half of the message, swore under his breath, and left for home.

⁂ TWENTY-SEVEN

Stanley Beltz had been up half the night, his brain jammed with facts and names and figures, his stomach rumbling with indigestion. His legs twitched. He turned on the bedside lamp and tried reading McBain's new book. When he couldn't concentrate, he picked up the week-old issue of Time and struggled through a boring column on commodities fraud, hoping it would wear him out. It only made him angry.

Verna Lake's murder was still his number one problem, and too much time was going by. After the first week, the trail gets cold. And the Markham incident was puzzling and depressing. One key suspect now knocked out of the box, the other mournfully lost in an endless and painful childhood.

He picked up the manila folder from the table, removed the charcoal drawing and studied the figure again, still hoping it would provide a clue, any clue, as to why Verna had drawn it. The strokes hurried, broad and rough, the piece of charcoal at one point breaking off, leaving a black smudge.The face was indistinguishable, the features blurred and incomplete. Why didn't she finish it?

The picture was trying to tell him something, he was certain of that, but he couldn't hear the words.

Maybe he was hungry. He slipped on old slippers and padded his way to the kitchen. When he turned on the light, the mess was brilliantly illuminated, and Beltz felt a sudden twinge of guilt.

"How can you possibly live like this, Stanley?" He could almost hear Lily's voice resounding from the walls. "My pride and joy, this kitchen. And it's going to stay that way. Like a stage set. No crumbs on the counters, no dirty dishes in the sink."

He looked at the dishes spilling over the drain rack. At least he'd brought his dishes in from the den. He wasn't a complete slob. The weekend would be a good time to clean it up.

He opened the fridge. Nothing on the shelves except two cans of beer and a jar of sweet gherkins. Rummaging in the cabinets, he finally found an old box of matzos and a jar of peanut butter and settled at the kitchen table with yesterday's paper.

His house had its own set of creaks and groans, especially in the middle of the night. He and Lily had moved into the small, two-bedroom bungalow after the children married. The second bedroom was his study, so cluttered with books and stuffed folders of current and past cases that Lily had long ago given up trying to keep it in order. She had thrown her hands up in disgust, closed the door, and told him she wouldn't step foot in it again; he could play in his own sand-pile. And he knew where every grain of sand was located, he shouted back.

Her garden in back was her favorite spot. He had kept up with the flowers the first year after her death, fertilizing and spraying faithfully, but this past summer had been too hot and too hectic. The garden lay neglected and withered now, and the howling wind outside was a portent of snow, which would cover it all up anyway, and he wouldn't have to look at it again until next spring.

Later on this morning, there was a meeting with Captain Sergosi to report any progress in the Lake murder. Sergosi was smarting under pressure from higher-ups, who were smarting under pressure from an aroused citizenry. And the press wouldn't let go.

It was a given; news is defined as bad news, and bad news sells papers. The honest person who returns a wallet or the guy who stops to give CPR to a heart-attack victim makes the last page, if at all.

He remembered when Sergosi had his lieutenant's job, and he, Beltz, had been a rookie patrolman. He'd shot a man fleeing from the scene of a crime. The guy had dropped like a stone and lay half dead in the street. An old man, that's what had shocked Beltz, so old; Jesus, eighty if he was a day, his wooly gray hair matted with blood. Beltz had expected a punk kid, pockets full of money from the A & P cash register. Instead, the old man had forty-seven cents in his pocket. Is that all life is worth, he had asked himself then, tears streaming down his face.

Lily tried to console him, his rabbi quoted proverbs from the Midrash and the Talmud: "The cause of his death was life, my boy, not you;" "Life is a passing shadow;" "All of life is a war;" but the counseling did nothing to assuage his guilt, and he handed Sergosi his shield.

"What are you, some kind of keystone cop?" the lieutenant had bellowed, kicking shut his office door. "We're cops because we feel something more than the average slob about our fellow man. We take an oath to serve and protect, and goddam it, if you've forgotten that, you don't deserve to wear that uniform. I told you like I told the brass and the press; you shouted to stop, and the guy didn't stop. So you shot him. What do you want, for me to hold your hand the rest of your life? Now take that shield and get out of here. And ponder my words good, for Christ's sake. Get your head screwed on right. If you still can't handle it, then I'll take your shield!"

In time the case disappeared from the front pages, and Beltz resumed his beat. When the old black man died a few weeks later, he relived the anguish of taking a human life, but remembered Sergosi's parting shot after that first meeting: "You're a cop, goddamn it, and if you can't bite, don't bare your teeth."

He only wished now that he could repay him with a break in this case, something positive, a bone to throw for those screaming for his head.

He sighed, folded the paper, added his dish to the pile in the sink, and ambled off to get dressed.

The wood carving class at the Indian Center was well attended on Friday night. Young boys and girls and even a few adults sat around tables with their required tools. They worked in basswood, soap, and small blocks of beech and pine.

George Burning Tree stood at the front of the room showing them, with a small pen knife, how to begin cutting into the wood. Drawing a crude design of a seal on the blackboard,he told them to copy and then try to carve it out of their block of wood.

When Beltz walked in, the Chief looked up briefly, showed no sign of recognition, then resumed his instruction.

Beltz was fascinated as George deftly whittled at the block, his strong hands making dexterous strokes into the wood. When he'd completed the outline, he switched to a jackknife, large and sharp, rounding off the edges and sides. The students attempted to follow, but were still in the preliminary stages when he had completed his figure.

"Be patient," he urged them, "this will take time to learn. I learned it as a child. It comes easy to me."

Beltz liked his attitude with the group, giving them individual help, spending time with each one. He was impressed, too, with George's ability with the knife. It was as if the tool was an extension of his hand, the ease and grace an intrinsic knack. The detective realized he was not only watching an Indian sharing a lifelong knowledge with his city-bred brothers, he was watching a suspect in a murder case who had an inordinate ability with a lethal weapon.

Perhaps it was a mistake, coming here like this. His thinking about the Chief was now definitely biased. In a way, it was unfair.

When the class finished, the Chief walked over to Beltz.

"You want to enroll, Lieutenant?"

"I think I've learned enough tonight, Chief."

"You like my seal?"

"You did a good job. Looks like a miniature of a real one."

"You take this seal. It's my present to you."

"Oh, I couldn't do that."

"You take it from me as a keepsake of friendship."

Beltz caught the Chief's eyes, soft and slightly sad. "That's nice of you, Chief."

"We used to be friends once. Now you think maybe I did something bad, no longer a friend."

Beltz shifted his stance. "Well, that's the way it goes sometimes."

"Tell me Lieutenant Beltz, why are you here tonight? Did you want to see me use this?" He held out the jackknife.

"Maybe. You're good with it, that's for sure. And you're good with the kids too," he added.

"I like the kids. I was once a poor kid and I got help. I never forget the missionaries. I always pay back what I owe."

Molly hadn't answered her phone all day Friday. Now it was Saturday and Beltz had gone from eagerness, to worry, to downright anxiety for her well-being. He was also feeling hurt and neglected. After the day and most of the night together he was eager to see her again. He decided, finally, that if he didn't get hold of her by this afternoon, he would run out to Evanston as soon as he left the office.

When the desk phone rang, he lifted the receiver hoping it was Molly.

"Lieutenant Beltz? This is Pearl Minkoff. Remember me?"

"I remember," he said, disappointed. "Verna's nice landlady."

"Yes. Well, sir, I hate to bother you, but I started to worry last night when I realized I might have made a mistake about something."

"A mistake? About what, Mrs. Minkoff?"

"You see there was this nice lady, she came to see me last week sometime, and she wanted to know about Verna. So we sat down and had a nice talk and tea and..."

"Mrs. Minkoff, what was the lady's name?"

"Mrs. Fast. I remember her name because it was the same as my mother's. A pretty name. Molly, I mean. Old fashioned, like mine. You just don't hear..."

Beltz gripped the receiver tightly. "You say she was there a week ago?"

"Yes, but wait a minute. She came back."

"When?"

"Thursday. In the morning. In fact, she tried to call you from here. I guess I told her something important and she tried to call you. She's sort of an amateur detective, isn't she?"

"What was it you told her, Mrs. Minkoff? That she thought was so important?'

"You know, it had just slipped my mind. She was asking me about a picture, had I seen a picture on the bedroom door. And I told her what I told you. That I hadn't seen it. And then she started asking about Verna's parents, and what kind of people they were. And I told her the only thing I really knew was what Verna had told me about her mother. How she was forever quoting the Bible. Whenever something important happened in their house, she always used some words from the Bible. Both the old testament and the new. Verna said sometimes she just wanted to go outside and scream.

"There was one phrase in particular her mother used all the time, ever since she was little. `Resist the devil and he will

183

flee from you.' I shouldn't have told her that. I should have told you. She left here in such a hurry. I hope she hasn't gone and done anything foolish."

❧ TWENTY-EIGHT

On Thursday morning, two days before Pearl's urgent phone call to Lieutenant Beltz, Molly reorganized the studio shelves and neatly repacked her camera bag. She loaded film in two cameras and tested her flash and strobe lights. She needed one more shot for a new client's layout, and shooting in the zoo was more fun than work. She'd be through by noon.

She locked the bag and thought about Stanley Beltz. Their day together had been a revelation, the night pure delight, his lovemaking patient and skilled.

Smiling at the memory, Molly walked slowly downstairs, the camera bag swinging from her shoulder. This afternoon, she would deliver Fuzzy's proofs. They were good; he could stop bugging her and she'd have some free time.

She passed the picture of her Aunt Dodie, at ninety-seven, still living a long, dull, and uneventful life. No great pleasure, no great pain. Not, Molly thought, like poor Verna Lake.

There was a sad life. Twenty-four years of loneliness and suffering, never at peace, confused with every facet of life where gender played a part, and realizing all this misery stemmed from one ghastly mistake: he was born in the wrong body.

And the final, painful surgery that changed the man to a woman, a drastic and irreversible mischief, was incomprehensible to Molly.

She looked down at her own body, curvaceous and indisputably feminine even in the baggy slacks and oversize shirt she had thrown on for the darkroom, and felt an overwhelming gratitude for the combination of good genes and whatever else nature had bestowed.

Molly realized, of course, that the emotional agonies of Verna Lake were far removed from her own life. Although, like everyone else, she was not completely free of problems, the wrenching pain of being born with the wrong equipment was far out of her ken. The chance of disfigurement from disease was about as close as she had ever come to that kind of thought process. To alter everything was an extreme that Molly could not deal with. Even to imagine it was too difficult.

Perhaps that was why Verne had become an artist, with some tangible means of expression. The paintings must tell a hundred stories, each one significant and illustrative of some deep-seated fear or desire.

The paintings! What had Stanley said about the sketch, a charcoal sketch hanging on a door? That no one had seen but him?

But Pearl Minkoff, at one time or another, must have seen some of the paintings Verna had worked on. Perhaps if she described them to Pearl, Molly might find a clue as to how Verna felt about the people in her life, some of whom were suspect. It was worth a try.

After phoning the landlady and setting up a time for her visit later this morning, Molly dressed, threw her camera bag in the car, and was on her way.

Pearl was happy to see Molly. She didn't have much company anymore, except for the reporters and photographers who had been bothering her and muddying up her kitchen floor. Molly was cheerful, unlike Pearl's women friends whose aches and pains and b.m.'s were the important topics of the day.

"Please come in. We'll have tea." Pearl said, ushering Molly into the parlor. "It looks like snow."

Then she frowned and shook her finger at Molly. "I hope you're not still poking that pretty nose of yours into poor Verna's death. You could get yourself in a heap of trouble. They don't know who the murderer is yet and he could be walking around free as a bird."

Molly followed Pearl into the kitchen and watched with amusement as the tea kettle blew its whistle and danced on the burner.

"No, I wouldn't interfere with police work," she said, "I've been good."

"I'm glad to hear that. Let's take the tea and go into the front room."

They chatted amiably, or rather Pearl chatted and Molly listened. The tea was hot and the cheese cake Pearl had defrosted in honor of Molly's visit was thick and creamy and covered with strawberries. Rich and fattening and Molly relished every mouthful.

"Did Verna ever have tea with you like this?" she asked.

"Oh yes. And that's what I miss. She was a nonstop talker, I guess like me, and we were always interrupting each other. And her jokes. They were the best. Funny. Really funny. Oh, I used to laugh. At my age, it's fun to laugh."

"I bet she showed you some of her paintings. I hear she was quite good."

"Was she ever! Especially the watercolors. Such beautiful scenes. The way she drew water, I tell you I wanted to jump right in! What a talent."

187

Pearl dropped her gaze and studied her tea cup for a moment. Then she looked at Molly. "You know, I try not to think about it, about her being a man, once. I will never understand such things."

Molly wanted to steer Pearl back to the paintings. "They say her oils and sketches were good too. And the charcoals? Did you ever see any of those?"

"I saw her picture of President Nixon once. That was in charcoal, I think. But she told me she had done that one in high school. It was good. Looked just like him. Evil."

Molly chuckled. "Anything else?"

Pearl thought, sipping her tea. "She had a group of pictures of children playing in the park. Like in the four seasons. And there was one I just loved. One of my prize roses last summer—Peace, it was—in my blue china vase. It was a grand picture. And Verna did tell me that one day I could have it." Pearl sighed. "I guess I'll never see it again."

"Why? Where is it?"

"I guess it's with all her things the Fitches took back with them last Sunday. What a sad time that was for them."

"Had you ever met them before?"

"No, never."

"Did she have any photos of them?"

"No. In fact, I never saw any photographs in her apartment at all. Now that I think of it, that must have been her way of kicking over any old traces."

Molly placed her cup in the saucer and looked closely at Pearl. "What was her mother like?"

"Sort of pale, pinched. I like that word. And that's what she was. You know, like lemon when you suck it."

"I know what you mean," Molly said. "Sour."

"That's right. Could be Verna felt that way too. She told me once how her mother spouted passages from the Bible for every occasion that came along. Birthdays, Thanksgiving, Christmas, any excuse to quote from The Book. There was one she used to hear over and over again. How she hated it."

"What was it?"

"'Resist the devil and he shall flee from you.' You know, I forgot about that. I never told the detective."

"Lieutenant Beltz, you mean?"

"Yes. Do you think it's important?"

Molly's heart raced with excitement; she took a quick sharp breath and stood up. "I sure do. Where's your phone?"

Minutes later, after Sergeant Neal had told her Beltz was out, Molly left her name and said she'd call him back.

"Shoot," she mumbled, returning to the living room. "He might be gone for the whole day. Mrs. Minkoff, thanks for the snack but I have to go."

On her way to Fort Wayne, Molly's head whirled with facts and conclusions. Right or wrong, they had to be sorted out and examined more carefully. And seeing that charcoal sketch Stanley had described could greatly simplify the process. What if she was right? What if…?

At this point, she almost turned back. Although Stanley had joked about giving her a shield, the fact remained that she did not have one. But because she had found the hand, she was intricately involved with Verna and her murder. And she had spent so much time researching facts and discovering clues, she was part of it now, and therefore had the right to see it through. And to do that, she must drive to the Fitch house in Fort Wayne.

Again she was stepping on Beltz's toes, treading into mucky waters without a life belt.

For Molly this was nothing new. She had acted on impulse most of her life. But never, she had to admit, with anything as serious as this.

❧ TWENTY-NINE

The sky was ominously dark and overcast when Molly finally drove up to the Fitch house. Barren trees nearby were bent almost double against the wind to hold their ground, and tangled, unkempt bushes scraped the wood siding and supports of the open porch.

As Molly walked to the front door, the wind slapped at her, and she pressed her bulky bag tightly against her body. She glanced quickly at the threatening sky, then mounted the steps.

The doorbell dangled by its wires. She knocked twice. A light inside the house indicated someone was home, but there was no answer. She knocked again.

"Mrs. Fitch?" she asked, as a small frail woman opened the door.

"Yes. Why? What do you want?" May Fitch said irritably.

"I hope you don't mind me barging in like this, but I'm Mrs. Fast from Chicago, and your son had shown me some of his paintings and I thought, I hoped you might be so kind as to sell me one. You see, I knew Verne from the Art Institute. I was a volunteer guide there. I'm so sorry about what happened."

Molly used Verna's former name, believing the mother might not want to acknowledge the sex change operation. She dreamed up this story on her way here, hoping it would gain her entrance to the Fitch house. It worked.

She studied the dishevelled-looking woman as they walked into the kitchen, her heart pinched at May's sallow face, her uncombed gray hair streaming like a broken nest down her back.

Nonetheless, May carried herself erect, shoulders straight, head high. The pupils of her puffy reddened eyes shifted about as if unsure where to light. Her housedress was filthy,the pocket bulging, the half belt hanging loose. In spite of the cold, the woman was barefoot.

Mrs. Fitch insisted that her guest have a cold drink after her long journey. Molly was chilled to the bone and would have preferred hot tea or coffee, but no choice was offered.

The kitchen was in complete disorder; dirty dishes and pots piled in the sink, condiment tins strewn over the counter top as though they had dropped from a cabinet and left where they had fallen. A broken egg, shell and all, lay on the floor near the refrigerator. The mess was a shocking contrast to the kitchen table, which was covered by a white lace tablecloth. Neat place settings for three were illuminated by a flickering candle in a glass holder. Molly wondered if the Fitches were expecting company.

"So you knew my boy at the Art Institute. He was a handsome boy, wasn't he?" Mrs. Fitch reached for Molly's hand. "My Verne, he sure looked the part, all right. A big Chicago artist, always dressed so smart. Sophisticated, they say. When I saw him last time, he was all decked out in those tight jeans they wear and a big sweatshirt. He even wore a matching cap on his head like I've seen in the movies. I hardly recognized him."

"Yes," Molly said, "every time I saw him, he was dressed in good taste."

"I always knew he would be successful." May's cheeks flushed. "But Carl, he never liked to see his son drawing. He

191

always thought it was a waste of time. Thought he should be helping him in the field, learning the ways of a farm so he could take over some day."

May's eyes brimmed with tears and she tried to blink them back. "But my Verne, he knew what he wanted. And I was all for it. Be strong and of good courage for the Lord thy God is with thee, I told him many a time."

"I'm sure that was good advice," Molly said softly, finally pulling her hand free. "The pictures?" she reminded May. "I'd love to see them now."

"Of course, I nearly forgot. Come with me."

May led the way into the little room behind the kitchen and Molly saw the red bloody figure of Jesus hanging on the wall. She shuddered at the forbidding thing, not knowing what to make of it. The man on the cross had always seemed beatific and benevolent to her, a symbol of worship and adoration. This one was malevolent, a thing from a black and bloody sabbath.

"They're right here," May said, "I keep them all together, just as he left them." She stroked them tenderly, as though a bit of Verne still remained on the black vinyl cover.

"Was there a particular one you wanted?" she asked.

Molly shook her head. "No, I liked so much of his work. There was a landscape. I don't know whether he sold it or not, but I'd love to own it. Could I just look through this collection and choose something?"

May looked doubtful. She seemed to be weighing Molly's suggestion, then decided to allow it.

"Go ahead," she said, releasing the precious possession, "but be careful. Don't get them dirty."

Molly began to examine the pictures one by one, her eye enchanted by the skillful use of color and line, the realistic still lifes and funny caricatures. The picture of the pig made her laugh. Mrs. Fitch never budged from her position nearby. It made Molly uneasy, but she couldn't very well ask the woman to leave.

She found a few charcoal sketches, but where was the prophet Beltz had described? He must have taken it with him when he came here. She was disappointed. It was the very thing she had come to see.

"Didn't find anything?" May asked, "with all those pretty pictures there?" Her brow furrowed as the question formed on her lips. "Why did you come?"

Molly realized she'd better make a choice. "I do love this one," she said, ignoring the woman's abrupt change of attitude. "May I buy it?" She held up a pastel landscape.

"I guess so." May's expression was now openly hostile. "If you can afford my price."

"How much do you want?"

"Two hundred dollars. There were funeral expenses, you know." She said this as if justifying an exorbitant amount.

Molly knew if she accepted right away, Mrs. Fitch might be suspicious. If she dickered with her, she might anger the woman, or worse, insult her.

"That's a bit steep, but I'll take it. I'll write you a check."

"No checks," May snapped, her voice unexpectedly harsh. "I want cash. I don't run to banks every day."

"Mrs. Fitch, I don't normally carry two hundred dollars around with me."

"Then you can't have the painting."

"Well then, thanks anyway. It's getting late. I'll be leaving now."

"No."

"No? What do you mean, no."

"Just what I said. You can't leave."

May's eyes glittered. She seemed distracted. First she clasped her hands and reverently looked up to the Jesus figure, mumbling under her breath. Then she seemed to gather strength and grabbed Molly's arm.

"Hast thou found me, O mine enemy?" May said softly, breathing the words into Molly's face.

"I'm not your enemy, Mrs. Fitch." Molly tried to free herself. "I only wanted to own one of Verne's paintings. That's the only reason I'm here. Maybe this wasn't a good time to come. I'll return again when you're feeling better."

"I feel fine. It's Carl who's sick. You want to see Carl? Of course you do."

The woman's grip tightened, and she pushed Molly back through the kitchen and into the parlor. There in the middle of the floor was the huddled form of a man, lying face down, as though he had pitched forward clutching his chest.

"That's Carl. He doesn't feel very good. He's been like that since this morning. Hasn't moved, hasn't asked me for anything." She flashed a mean smile and said, "He has come to smite him for his sinful act."

"Is he dead?" Molly cried. "Did you call someone? A doctor? The police?"

"No. The Lord told me to leave him there, for he has been wicked."

Molly pulled away and ran to Carl. "Maybe we can help him," she said, reaching for a pulse. His skin was ice-cold. There was no pulse. "Mrs. Fitch, your husband is dead. We have to do something about this. I'll call the police. Where's your phone?"

May Fitch moved to her husband's body, kneeled down, and began a mournful keening in a shrill, high-pitched voice.

Molly was moved by the woman's grief, almost forgetting her earlier hostility. She waited in respectful silence.

Suddenly May threw back her head and emitted a hideous cackling laugh, teeth bared, cords standing out in her neck. Tears squeezed out of her tightly shut eyes and slithered down her cheeks. Then, as suddenly as it started, it stopped, and she stared at Molly with eyes like black glass beads.

"Some evil beast," she shouted, as if Molly were deaf, "evil...evil...EVIL!...hath devoured him."

This hysteria, and the dead body in the middle of the floor, filled Molly with sinister foreboding. This house reeked of violence and demonic spirit, and for the first time since entering, she was frightened.

May's biblical rantings surely pointed to Carl as Verna's killer. But she wasn't convinced that sticking around to learn the truth would be worth it.

"Mrs. Fitch..."

"Call me May," the woman said, an abrupt change turning her sweet and girlish. "May. May. May!" she repeated childishly. "'The prettiest girl in May,' my mother used to say, over and over and over again. Like the hurdy-gurdy in the town square. And the monkey danced..."

Her eyes wandered as she turned and twisted, floating, it seemed, on another plane.

"May, the phone. Where is it?"

May didn't hear Molly. She was immersed in dreams and images, part of time past and time never lived. "Poor Carl, you didn't listen. Vengeance is mine. I will repay, saith the Lord. Bad Carl. Poor Verne...no more pretty pictures."

She began to sob, great heaving gasps rending her frail body, the sounds of grief like the cries of a wounded animal. When the tears ceased, she sat back on her heels and stared ahead, her eyes unfocused, glazed over, and Molly decided this was her chance to get out.

She edged her way slowly along the wall, almost reaching the front door, when May's head suddenly snapped around. She saw Molly and her face contorted with rage, like a death's head under the stretched and swollen skin.

Reaching into her pocket, May pulled out a long, black-handled butcher knife and lunged forward, clawing at the air. Molly tried to dodge her but wasn't quick enough.

The woman had incredible strength, fueled by a blind and fancied paranoia toward the intruding lady from Chicago, and, like a spoiled child abusing a stuffed toy, pushed and shoved Molly, throwing her onto a wooden chair.

"Let me go, Mrs. Fitch."

"May. Call me May."

195

"May. If Carl has done something wrong, the police must be informed." Molly was angry, yet her whole body trembled from the shocking assault.

"Sent to spy out the land?" May hissed. "Sit forever and dwell on it. Sit for ever...for ever...for ever..."

May kept repeating the words, running from window to window and yanking the tie-backs from their white plastic brackets. As she executed her erratic dervish, Molly again made a dash for the door.

It was no use. The dead-bolt had been thrown and May had the key.

"Come back, Miss Nosyparker," May called, "you can't get out. Sit in the chair like a good girl, and visit with me." Her voice had turned whiney. "You want to know about Carl? Just sit quietly and I'll tell you."

Molly stared at the knife in May's hand, unable to believe this was happening. She had never faced a weapon, especially one like the knife in May's hand, never been threatened in any way. Totally unprepared for this turn of events, she was flustered momentarily, unable to react. Yet it was clear the woman was utterly mad, her mouth gone slack, dried spittle clustered at the corners. At any moment, and without further provocation, May could plunge the knife into her unwelcome guest.

Seeking to pacify her, and waiting until she could make her move to get out, Molly returned and sat down. "May, what about Carl? What did he do?"

"That's for you to ask and for me to tell you. Or not."

The sing-song voice took on a strident edge. "Put your hands in back of you!"

Molly struggled, resisting the old woman by beating at her with clenched fists and kicking at her shins. But when May slid the knife across her throat, knicking her cheek with the sharp tip and drawing blood, Molly gave up.

May pulled the corded tie-backs tightly around Molly's wrists, then tied them to the back of the chair. With Molly securely pinioned, the woman tip-toed to her husband's body on the floor. Kneeling over him, she bobbed up and down, moving in time to some inner and inaudible rhythm, the words coming from her lips in a low, murmuring cadence. "Yet a little sleep, a little slumber, a little folding of the hands to sleep. Yet a little sleep…"

To Molly, it sounded like a mother crooning her baby to sleep. Poor demented thing, she thought, and shivered. Deadly prayers. The baby is dead.

❧ THIRTY

Tied to the chair, Molly could only watch May praying over her husband's body and wonder how long Carl had been dead. She also suspected that May killed him, and if so, she was perfectly capable of doing Molly in too. Her eyes searched the dark room, looking for any possible exit from this evil house. The windows were shut tight, shades pulled. She knew the front door was locked. Through the rear doorway she saw another room beyond, dark, and too far away. Even if she could find a way out, Molly had to free herself first.

If May kept at her lamentations and Molly could find something to rub against the binding ropes, she had a chance. But she'd have to move the chair. And this would make noise. The only answer was for May to tire and fall asleep. And Molly must stay awake.

Hours passed as she watched and listened, the woman keeping up the steady, maddening litany of religious zeal. But there was no doubt that her voice was losing strength, her body beginning to sag against Carl's bulk. Molly waited, like a hunter waits for his prey, patient and unhurried.

When the sound of May's even breathing signaled her fall into a deep sleep, Molly played the chair along, inch by inch, one leg at a time, in painfully slow motion, toward the metal gallery rail of the desk.

The distance seemed the length of a football field, but in reality, was only about four feet. She nudged the chair, waited, nudged it again, waited. When she reached the desk, she paused until certain May would not hear the scraping sound.

The position was awkward. She would have to turn the chair around. Once that was done, she worked her hands up near the sharp metal edge, then began the jerky uneven sawing at the rope.

With her heavy coat still buttoned, the maneuver was difficult. She felt clumsy and burdened. Her arms ached, her back with each movement was stinging with pain. She was perspiring even though the room was ice-cold, and rivulets of sweat ran down her arms and legs.

As she tried leaning closer, concentrating on the task, a voice whispered in her ear. "Would this help?"

It was May, standing next to Molly, offering her the knife. A twisted grimace distorted her features.

"Here, take it. Don't you want it? What are you waiting for? Oh, are you tied up? What a shame. You can't have it, then. You can't hold it that way. Maybe this way."

She raised her arm, the steel blade glinting in the dim light, and Molly felt the squeezing, strangling grip of cold terror.

"All that work. Tsk, tsk, tsk," May clucked sympathetically, "and you didn't even make one cut on the ropes. You're a naughty little girl. I'll have to punish you."

Frail as she was, May dragged the imprisoned Molly to the radiator near the window and tied one chair leg to the metal pipe. Somewhere in the back of Molly's brain loomed the realization that May's incredible strength seemed to have a focus, a goal, the point growing and expanding to some monstrous and unremitting resolve.

"There, that better? Nice and cozy?"

"Mrs. Fitch," Molly said evenly, "I have no quarrel with you. I won't do you any harm. Why don't you let me go?"

"Go? Go where? Where would you go? To Sodom? Is that where you live? No, you stay with Carl and me. It's too cold outside for someone like you, used to the warmth, eh?" She gave a cackling laugh and slapped her thigh. "Get it? The warmth? To hell, you'll go! You hear me? To hell!"

Then she turned and whirled on Molly. "We'll all have dinner. You and me and Verne...and Carl. A nice pork roast and potatoes and pumpkin pie. And you can say grace. We'll look through the Bible together, you and me. Pick something real nice, something fitting."

With that, May left the room.

Molly could hear the sounds of pots and pans clanking, the rattling of dishes. In a short time, the woman returned bearing a plate in each hand which she set before Molly on the floor.

One raw egg, its yoke runny and broken, swam in a sea of rust-colored water on the floral china. On the other plate, a mound of spoiled chopped meat, green and moldy around the edges.

"The Lord tells us to feed the hungry traveler, so eat!"

Molly took a deep breath, and said, "Mrs. Fitch, if you would release my hands, I will be able to eat your delicious dinner. I know you've spent a lot of time preparing it."

"Miss Smarty Pants, you'll find a way. That should be an easy task for you. Your feet are free." May laughed, an unmerry and raucous noise that affected Molly more than the knife. "I once saw a woman on television who had no hands.She ate with her feet!" May giggled with delight.

In spite of her calm exterior, Molly seethed with anger at the ludicrous situation, her mind struggling to find any possible means of escape. She knew in this she was alone. By foolishly not telling anyone she was going to Fort Wayne, there would be no frantic phone calls, no one, in fact, to come after her.

Maybe Stanley had been right to lecture her about amateur detecting. So why didn't she listen. Stubborn, know-it-all Molly Fast, the smart-ass widow from Evanston, in a mess now that could cost her her life. To die so ignobly in this house from hell.

"My dear, my dear, you're not eating. You must fuel your body to keep up your strength."

"Mrs. Fitch, release my hands."

May stood, one hand on her hip, the other gripping the knife, and bestowed on Molly a benign expression.

"You haven't tried to eat with your feet yet. Everyone must try something once. I always said that to little Verne. Try it once. If at first it doesn't work, try it another way."

Molly looked at her feet, clad in black leather boots zipped to the knee, and picked up on May's words. "Pull my boots off, and I'll try to use my toes."

May cocked her head as she thought over the suggestion. "Clever, Miss Butinsky, aren't you? You want me to put down the knife, eh?"

"If you want me to eat, my boots must be off." As Molly spoke, she felt the crusted blood cracking on her cheek. The scene may resemble a low-budget horror movie, but her dread was abject. She could feel the pounding of her heart, and under the heavy coat, her flesh began to crawl.

A light glowed in May's hollow eyes and she placed the knife's blade between her teeth. She bent down and as she began unzipping the boots, Molly suddenly kicked up her legs, knocking May off balance.

The woman scrabbled to her feet, screaming, the piercing cry starting on a high note and descending the scale like the weird trembling voice of a screech owl. She stretched out her arms and glared at Molly, in that moment looking exactly like a prophet of the Old Testament exhorting the Sodomites to cease their sinning or God would wreak His vengeance and destroy them.

Molly gasped, her suspicions now shockingly confirmed;

May's pose was identical to the charcoal drawing Beltz had seen on Verna's door.

With heart-stopping horror, she watched May retrieve the knife and arc it downward with a whoosh of air to rest against her throat.

"You try that again," May snarled, "and I'll cut off your toes one by one."

Molly sat rigid, not daring to blink, then placed her stockinged feet on the floor after May removed her boots.

"No! Don't do that!" May shouted, "put off thy feet from the place whereon they touch, for it is holy ground."

"Where can I put my feet?" Molly yelled. "What do you want from me? You said to pick up the plate. I can't do that without touching the floor."

"Your feet must be bare, like mine. It's blasphemous if they're not. Off with your stockings!"

"They're not stockings, they're tights. And I can't take them off unless my hands are free."

The old woman smiled, a lop-sided grimace that added a chilling accent to her threat. "Then I'll have to cut them off."

With that, she kneeled and slashed off the bottom of the tights. She was careless, the knife piercing Molly's skin on both ankles. They bled.

"Now, Miss Peeping-Tom, let's see you do it. Your meat loaf is getting cold. Eat!" she ordered.

Molly curled her toes over the plate of meat and slid it toward the chair, knowing she would never be able to accomplish the contortions necessary to bring it up to her mouth.

Purposely, she pushed the plate back and had to start over again, playing for time. May enjoyed the entertainment, giggling every so often at her prisoner's predicament.

Finally, exasperated as Molly dropped the plate again, May snatched it from the floor and threw it across the room. It crashed against the wall, china splintering, bits of meat and brown liquid dribbling down the gray painted surface like clotted blood.

Quivering with rage, May leaned down, so close Molly could smell her sour breath. "Why did you come here? You, a stranger in a strange land."

She rose suddenly and stood upright. "Be sure your sin will find you out."

As she walked away, gliding as if skating on ice, she stopped to bend over Carl's body and pat it tenderly.

"Who is on my side? Who?" She waited expectantly. When there was no response, she shrugged and left the room.

Alone now, Molly was able to let down her guard. She relaxed in the chair, rotating her head to ease the tension, and wondered what time it was. She had arrived at the house around six o'clock Thursday night, and figured it must now be at least three a.m. Friday. She was hungry, she was thirsty, and she had to urinate. And she had to think of a way out.

There was no one else here. And May was small and frail.The knife posed a problem, especially in the hands of a crazy old woman blinded by grief and blinded...Blinded!

The idea came suddenly to Molly, clear and feasible even as she saw a shadow moving near the food-stained wall. She blinked.

Another seemed to join it, both shadows now hunched over Carl's body on the floor. After a moment, there was a sudden rush of wind and an ear-splitting yowl as the black tomcat flew into Molly's lap.

Not a split second later, the orange tabby landed on her shoulder, its long sharp claws digging into her neck.

With the scream rising in her throat, Molly twisted against the binding ropes and hissed at the cats, fighting them with every frenzied push of her upper body and kicking out with her feet.

The orange tabby arched free, its claws taking bits of Molly's skin as it jumped to the floor. The black tom followed, screaming its displeasure at the orange cat as he chased it out of the room.

Hot tears sprang from Molly's eyes, and she batted her lids rapidly to stop them. Involuntary though they were, the tears were unwelcome and ill-timed. Forget the damn cats, she muttered angrily to herself, and concentrate on escape.

ᴓ THIRTY-ONE

During the dark hours of the morning the wind picked up, and somewhere in the house, a loose shutter banged against a window, sounding a monotonous tapping like a mechanical drum. Off in the distance a dog barked, and occasionally the headlights of a passing automobile on the road streaked across the shaded windows.

The house was silent. Molly's feet were numb with cold. Her wrists hurt from the ropes digging into the flesh. May's repeated stabs at Molly had shredded the upper part of her black coat, and it hung in pieces around her shoulders.

Some time during the night, her full bladder had let go, and she shivered now in the wet clothes. Daylight allowed her to see clearly. It was a weary room, filled with cheap oversized furniture, undoubtedly bought from a catalogue house years ago. An ancient and soiled friezé couch stoutly sat between two tall double-hung windows. The shades, water-stained and yellowed with age, were pulled to the sills. Flanking the couch were two matching early American end tables, their lamps odd and clumsy, obviously hand made from tree limbs. Green paper shades with perforated designs perched atop each lamp like ill-fitting hats.

A cobbler's bench was placed against the wall, and it was here the plate of food had landed the night before. It had dried to a mottled brown mess, and Molly quickly looked away.

Two scarred ladder-back chairs with torn cane seats rested beside the fireplace. Ashes spilled from the grate onto the cement hearth which was blackened randomly from charring cinders.

In the center of the room Carl still lay on a small Chinese rug, its pattern and color long since faded. The scene was dismal and untidy, and Molly couldn't help comparing it to the chic slick artificial sets with which her career had so long been associated. Props, she thought. What a spread these would make, and enough here for a lifetime of gag shots.

Molly suddenly heard heavy footsteps climbing the porch stairs, followed by a loud, persistent knocking on the front door.

May came running from a room beyond the kitchen. "You make one sound, Miss Twinkle-Toes, and my knife will shred more than your coat."

Molly stared, but said nothing.

May cried out, "Who is it?"

"Sheriff Boone, Miz Fitch. Come for Carl."

"Carl?" she yelled through the door.

"He should-a been at the Village Hall this morning. Supposed to sign that state highway commission paper for the new road. He's late. They need his signature for the petition."

May was unprepared for this curve thrown her by the sheriff. Molly could see the erratic movements of her hands beating at her head as she desperately tried to think of what to say.

"Didn't say nothing to me about that," she bellowed. "Gone to see his sick brother in Jasper. Don't know when he's coming back. Maybe next week."

"That sure is strange, Miz Fitch. We were countin' on Carl."

"Well, flesh and blood, Sheriff. Nothing stronger than that."

"You got kin visitin', Miz Fitch?"

"No, why?"

"This car out here...got Illinois plates. With an Evanston sticker. You got kin in this here Evanston?"

"No kin," she called out quickly. "A friend of Verne's come for the funeral."

"Still here?"

"Yes. For a few days."

Molly could hear most of the conversation and knew it was the sheriff. If only she could attract his attention without crying out. Her only chance was to tip herself over in the chair with a big enough noise to make him curious.

But because one chair leg was tied to the radiator pipe, it could not be tipped. She did the next best thing by leaning the chair back against the radiator and banging it repeatedly.

"What's that noise, Miz Fitch?"

"Just the wind. Been shaking the shutters all morning. Bye, Sheriff," May called.

"Want me to check on it for you, with Carl away and all?"

"No, I'll get Verne's friend to take care of it."

With the sheriff's footsteps going down the stairs, Molly's frenzy increased, her body jumping with the chair as she whacked it back and forth against the radiator. God damn it...hear me! Why can't you hear me.

The noise inside the room was loud, but she knew it had to go through the walls and tightly shut windows, and the odds against that were great. But she kept up the thumping and banging, knowing all the while it was no use.

When the sheriff's car pulled out of the driveway, Molly's heart sank.

May turned to her, livid with rage. "An ox goeth to the slaughter..."

As the mad woman approached, Molly yelled, "Wait! Mrs. Fitch...wait! I'm Verne's friend, remember?"

May froze, confused.

"We were good friends. You said so yourself. To the sheriff. I came here to be with you. To help you during this difficult time. Verne was my friend."

"Friend?" May's eyes rolled in her head; she seemed to be searching the air for affirmation of Molly's statement.

"Verne's friend," Molly repeated.

"Verne's friend, yes." May smiled sweetly. "Then I won't kill you...now."

"Why would you kill me if I'm Verne's friend?"

But May did not hear. She walked over to her husband's lifeless body and snuggled close.

"You hear that, Carl?" she whispered. "Verne's friend is here to see us. It's so sad now, isn't it? Without Verne." She shook her head. "But you know, he that diggeth a pit shall fall into it. Poor Verne...poor Verne..."

Mercifully, May and her cats did not appear again until late that night. The woman had wandered off behind the kitchen shortly after the sheriff had gone, and Molly had been left to her own thoughts. She was faint with hunger and thirst, and after May's midnight appearance, asked repeatedly for water. But the woman ignored her, floating in and out of the room like a wraith.

Molly kept working on her plan, thinking out alternative moves with every possible scenario. But the success of her plan hinged on getting her bag. Just when she thought of a way, she'd doze off, then awaken to realize she'd forgotten it.

And what about Stanley Beltz. Was he worried about her, was he calling? Did he miss her? Maybe he didn't miss her at all. He'd said he hoped they could be together again, soon. He was nice, a different kind of man. That night they had shared together had been so beautiful. Like two young kids—so impetuous—be nice to be in his arms right now.

She shook those thoughts out of her head and tried to stay awake. Think, you dumb broad. Concentrate. Or you're going to wind up sliced meat for that nut case's supper.

The squat mahogany mantle clock helped Molly keep track of the time and passing days. She knew it was seven on Saturday morning when she awoke, the rotting smell of Carl's body strong and acrid in her nostrils. She gagged and coughed and tried to think of something sweet growing in her summer garden.

Her brain was foggy and disorganized, but with great effort, she began to count the hours of her ordeal. Thursday night to Saturday morning...thirty-seven hours? Could it be? Sitting, tied up, stiff and bruised and cut, for thirty-seven hours?

Face it, Molly, no one is going to save you. You're on your own, baby. Forget the white knight or the Lone Ranger. And where the hell is May?

The early morning light was dim and grayed over, more like twilight than the onset of a new day. Maybe it had started to snow. She couldn't tell. Snow is white and clean, soft when you pack it or roll it, or shovel it to make a neat path. It's nice to sit in front of a fire when it snows outside. Drinking champagne. Or nibbling on popcorn or potato chips. Blue and red flames dancing together like ballerinas on a floodlit stage. Dressed in warm satin pajamas, with Stanley reading from Browning's sonnets—then they could fool around...

A crashing noise, startling in the grim silence, jerked up Molly's head. Her eyes flew open. She saw not two but four huge cats running into the room. The crash had awakened them, and they scattered everywhere, yowling and hissing and ready to strike. The black tom sat at Molly's feet, its yellow eyes never leaving her face.

"Well, aren't you the lucky one," May whined jealously, "King Herod seems to be giving you all his attention. But don't take him seriously. He's fickle."

Molly's blood ran cold. She was sweating profusely. Her skin crawled, but she would not utter a sound. May ran to the cat. "Scat, King Herod! To hell with you! No breakfast!"

The cat hissed and arched its back, and for a moment, Molly thought it would jump at May, claws bared. But it only skulked away to a corner, settling its big black body into a graceful curve.

May turned to Molly. "Pity! Pity! And I dropped your delicious breakfast. Nice hot oatmeal with butter and cream. Now you'll have to wait until lunch. We're going to have pot roast with my special potatoes and gravy. And if you're very good, there's some vanilla ice cream in the freezer."

Molly knew the broken dish had been empty. No food spilled from it. Only pieces of china lay scattered about.

"Now I won't have to wash it," May said gleefully. "I suppose you wear gloves when you wash dishes, huh?" Contempt curled her mouth into an ugly smear. "You have nice nails? Let's see."

She walked to Molly and fussed with the bindings on her wrists.

"Oh, pretty polish, pink, not red like…"

Molly lifted her head and murmured, "Not like what, May?"

The woman peered down at her captive. "My little Verne was left-handed, did you know that? And I'd slap his hand all the time, whenever he used it. The left hand is the devil's hand, I told him. And I tried to make him change. I even let those nails grow so they would get in the way. But he bit them off. He'd bite and bite until he made those fingers bleed."

She shook her head. "My good little Verne was so bad, sometimes. I painted the tips with iodine. It burned, it made him cry. And then I'd whip him. Oh, he cried plenty then.

But he kept biting those nails. Never bit the other hand, though."

May turned away, then looked back at Molly, her gaze steady, her mind momentarily free of its dark meandering journeys. "For all this, His anger is not turned away, but His hand is stretched out still."

Encouraged by May's return to reality, Molly tried to keep her there. "Where's that from, May?"

"From Isaiah. From the good book. All truths can be found in the good book. My father used to say that. He was a man of the cloth, you know."

"Tell me about him."

May smiled. "He was a holy man, a man of honor, who brought the truth like mounds of riches to his parishioners. His church was small, and he watched over it all by himself after mother died. Late into the night I could see him polishing the wooden pews and mending the altar cloth. He was a carpenter too, you know, could fix anything. He tried to teach little Verne, spent hours with the boy, noble, he was, and God-fearing. Pure in heart and soul."

She sighed, a long quivering sigh, like a child after a crying spell. "He shall return no more to his house, neither shall his place know him any more."

"He sounds like a wonderful man." Even as she mouthed the words, Molly tried desperately to remember her scheme: escape, something about her camera bag...

"I used to read to him all the time. But I have no one to read to, now that Carl is gone. Well now, why don't I read to you?"

With little slapping steps on the wood floor, May scurried to the bookshelf and pulled down a big worn leather-bound Bible.

Think, Molly...the bag...

"Let's see, where shall I begin?" May said cheerfully, pulling a chair alongside Molly. She settled herself, smoothing out her dirty housedress as if it were a satin ball gown, letting the untied sash flutter gracefully to the floor.

She opened the Bible.

"We'll begin," she said, flashing a self-satisfied grin, "in the beginning."

ঽ THIRTY-TWO

Molly's strategy blurred in and out of focus as May read chapter and verse from the Bible, her voice droning on, ebbing and flowing like waves on a faraway shore. Now and then May would rise from the chair and read right into Molly's ear. The sound reverberated, sliding between bass and treble, loud and then inaudible, and May would smile wickedly, reseat herself, and resume reading. This amalgam of sounds and words confused Molly and muddled her thoughts, forcing her to start all over again.

She was floating, entering and exiting a long narrow tunnel. At the end of the tunnel she could see herself sitting on a chair, bound hand and foot. Her limbs were numb and she had long since forgotten about hunger, the sharp pangs in her stomach finally gone, leaving a dull constant ache. Her thirst was intense and she kept biting her lips and tongue to salivate. Her head throbbed with pain, monumental and agonizing pain that never seemed to let up, burning hot and feverishly, as if this, apart from her shivering body, had been thrust into an oven.

From her neck down, the feeling was reminiscent of her worst childhood memory: after playing in the snow on a raw winter day, she cried to her mother that she was cold and wanted to come in. Her mother hadn't heard the cries, and by the time a neighbor brought her inside, her hands and feet were frozen. They healed in time, but she had never forgotten the incident, and now and then in this hellish experience, thought she was three years old again.

But these tricks of her brain alternated with streaks of bravado, when she would shout her defiance of May, choking out the words in a hoarse croak. May paid no attention, although after the fourth or fifth outburst, she began to stumble as she read, losing her place and her temper.

Now, Molly said to herself. Do it now or forget it.

"May, if you'll hand me my bag, I'll show you a picture of Verne. He gave it to me the day I saw his paintings. It's a lovely shot, May, with the sun shining down on his blond hair."

"What?" May's head snapped up from the page. She stared for a moment, her eyes wide with surprise. Her expression seemed to soften, but only momentarily. The stiff mask returned, her words coming out like cold spit.

"Don't you talk about my Verne. Don't you mention his name, filth like you. You don't deserve to breathe the same air…"

"I only wanted to share his picture with you, that's all. If you don't want to see it, forget it. But I would think a mother who has lost a son…"

"Quiet! Shut your mouth! What do you know about a mother and son."

"Plenty," Molly lied, courage returning like warmth after a hard winter. "I have a son. The same age as Verne. I love him more than anything in the world. If I were to lose him, and someone, even a stranger, had his picture, I would treasure it. You're a crummy mother, May."

The woman froze, turned to ice by Molly's scorn. Then her pale face suffused slowly with color and she rose from the chair and stood like an avenging demon over Molly.

214

"How dare you," she spat out, "how dare you call me that. My son adored me. He called me his angel, his precious. His Madonna!"

Molly threw her head back and laughed. "You've got to be kidding," she said. Her voice was hoarse. The dried skin around her mouth seemed to split open, and she could taste her own blood. "Then a mother like you, a saint, yet, wouldn't need any pictures. He's engraved in your mind, right May? I withdraw my offer. I'll keep the picture for myself."

May fell backward as if she had been struck. Her mask collapsed and she began to weep. "No, no. Please let me see it."

Molly shook her head. "Forget it, May."

"Please. I'll get your bag."

"It won't do any good. My hands are tied, remember?"

"I'll open your bag and get it out," May cried, already halfway across the room.

"You can't open it. It's locked. And you don't know the combination."

May picked up the camera bag which was closed tightly, the big combination lock dangling from the handles. Molly always locked it when taking it out of the house. The three cameras and flash attachments and strobe light were too valuable to carry around without even that small defense.

May brought it to Molly, struggling under the weight.

"Here. Open it."

"I can't. My hands are tied. Lots of luck, May."

The old woman wrestled with the problem, her features working, mirroring the effort. "All right. I'll untie you. But no tricks."

Molly's pulse skipped erratically as she brought all angles of the plan together in her mind.

1. 2. 3. 4. Do it, Molly, or get off the pot.

May took the knife from her pocket and cut the ropes.

"Wait," she said, drawing back, snatching up the bag and clutching it to her thin bosom. "I haven't finished my reading yet. When I'm through, you can show me the picture."

She sat on her chair, the bag in her lap, and placed the Bible on top. "Now you listen, and don't interrupt. I'll cut you to ribbons if you do. And I can slice this bag open, you know, so don't tempt me, Miss Fancy-Pants. God will provide Himself a lamb. He has done so before."

May's eyes looked heavenward, as though she were approaching the throne of God. "I have seen Him, you know," she said in a confidential tone to her prisoner, "and His voice was clear and for me alone. And I followed His instructions. I have always obeyed the Lord."

Her senses now fully alert, Molly targeted in on the word *lamb*. If it meant what she thought, the puzzle was missing only one piece.

But she had to be careful. The knife was a reality, and the woman was smarter than she thought.

She urged, "Tell me about the lamb, May."

May kept her eyes raised, fell to her knees, and in a voice vibrating with conviction, said, "Bone of my bones, flesh of my flesh...take now Thy son, Thine only son whom Thou lovest...and behold! The lamb! With long yellow hair and painted face...and long red nails."

As the woman raved on, she stood up, the book and bag lying on the floor. Unheeding, her impassioned fervor now blazing in unbound ecstasy, she did not see as Molly's foot slid over to the bag and pulled it back. May was unaware that Molly reached down, quickly dialed the lock, opened the zipper, and took out the strobe light.

Then May cried out, "Take her, my Lord, take her sinner's soul, take her sinner's body. Get out, Verne, run! The Lord will forgive. Only sinners dwell with the devil!"

She turned and stared straight into Molly's eyes. "I set my house in order, and now sorrow and sighing shall flee away." Her face twisted grotesquely; her eyes, no longer little glass beads, glittered like black diamonds, with a foul and virulent madness.

"And now you must die!"

Molly caught her breath. As May raised the knife high as her arm could reach, Molly aimed the strobe at May and pushed the button. The jagged white light flashed repeatedly, blinding May as she staggered backwards, the knife slipping from her fingers and clattering to the floor.

Molly stared, transfixed, only for a moment. Then, with a choked cry of triumph, she rose from the chair and stood on trembling legs, her fingers still pressing the button on the strobe. At the sound of splintering wood, she whirled, bathing the front door in a dazzling blaze of light as Stanley Beltz and Sheriff Boone burst into the house.

❧ THIRTY-THREE

"He was all I had. He was all I ever had."

May sat alert and stiff-backed on a chair. She had smoothed her hair with her hands, and the pale blush of color rising to her cheeks gave her a rested appearance. She stared straight ahead, not looking at either Lieutenant Beltz or Sheriff Boone, but her eyes were no longer feverish. She spoke slowly and seemed composed, submissive, her Job-like stoicism once again in command.

"He was my good boy who followed me, holding tight to my skirt, always helping me. The image of his grandfather, that sainted man.

"I came to see my boy, brought the ring with me, my father's ring. He wore it 'till the day he died. It was Verne's to wear now. I begged him. But he said no. I cried. I pleaded. But he could be mean and stubborn, like Carl.

"Standing there in that cap and those tight pants, glaring at me, his own mother. I grabbed his hand and slid the ring on his finger. That's when I saw the nails, the bright red color of sin, painted like a street slut.

"And she laughed and took off the cap and shook down the yellow hair. I screamed, 'Where's my Verne? What have you done to him?' She told me what she had done to Verne. And I was furious. This painted whore was not going to wear my father's ring. It was only for Verne.

"'Sinners dwell with the devil,' I told her, 'resist the devil and he shall flee from you.' I ran out of the house and walked the streets. I don't know for how long. And when I came back, this yellow-haired thief who took my son away was hanging a picture on the back of the door like nothing had happened.

"She talked soft words to me...'Mama,' she said, over and over to me...but I wasn't her mama...I was Verne's mama. And she took me by the arm and we went down the stairs, outdoors. The night air was cool, but the fires of hell were consuming me, trying to get me too.

"We stopped where there was nobody around. I could hear Verne calling to me...'Save me, Mama'...this woman just stood there, holding out her hand, yelling at me to take the ring...that I didn't know what my father was really like. Tried to tell me all those made-up lies about him...kept going on and on about bad things happening in that shed. How dare that cheap baggage talk about my father that way.

"And I remembered the knife Carl put in my purse when he waited with me at the bus station. He knew the big city was a bad place for a woman alone. He made this knife, you know, pretty black leather handle, hand stitched it himself, the blade as sharp as a honed scythe.

"I was in such a rage I yanked the knife out of my purse. I took back the ring, all right! I chopped off her hand! I chopped and chopped...and it finally fell off. Her screaming didn't fool me...she was bad! So I kept on stabbing her until she fell. For she that diggeth a pit shall fall into it. And I covered her over with all the dirt.

"Then I heard Verne's voice...'I'll come back to you, Mama...leave the ring. I'll wear it. I'll come back to you.' So I took the hand, the beautiful ring still on her finger, and wrapped it carefully...oh so tenderly, and dropped it in a garbage can where he could find it. You see? He finally listened to me. He's my good boy, my Verne.

"And that's what I told Carl. Poor Carl. Wicked Carl. He never believed in the Bible. He wouldn't believe me when I told him what this hussy had done to our little Verne. And he wouldn't believe me when I told him what I did to her. His eyes got all big and shiny, his face went all white. He stopped talking. Then he grabbed at his chest and fell over. Right there. As it is said in Ecclesiastes: `And the place where the tree falleth, there it shall be.'

"How many times I told that boy, as my sainted father used to say to me: `Resist the devil, and he shall flee from you.' Resist the...resist...re..."

Beltz carried Molly to the car, his arms tight around her. He placed her gently into the passenger side, pulled the blanket over her, tucked it under her chin, and pinned on a toy police badge he had in his pocket to give her as a joke.

The dark curtain of sky lifted as they drove back to the city, and the first snow of the season began to fall.

✺ THIRTY-FOUR

"Oh, it feels so good to be clean again," Molly said, stepping from the bathroom, wrapped in Beltz's robe and running her fingers through freshly washed hair. "That bath was actually therapeutic. I've never sat in a tub that long, but I can see why some people do it."

"I thought maybe you'd gone down the drain with the dirty water," Beltz said, chuckling, "and my robe has never looked so good."

He had been poking at the fire, trying to get his den warm before she was through bathing. The fire was now blazing. He closed the screen, and said, "Let's sit here until your hair is dry. Then I'll take you home."

"I don't think I can go home, Stanley, I don't want to be alone tonight. Can I stay with you?"

"Need you ask?" He hugged her to him. They sat quietly like this for a few minutes, then Molly said, "Can we have some more soup later?"

"I have more cans in the pantry. That's all I seem to have around here these days, soup and bagels."

"Stanley?"

"Molly?"

"Did you think it was May all along?"

"You're ruining my romantic moment," Beltz protested.

"I'll bring it back, don't worry. But I've got to know."

"Well," he said, giving in, "I had a hunch. Things Pearl told me, the drawing, it all started to come together. May was in denial about Verne's sex change, and that sort of clued me in at the beginning."

Molly listened intently, her teeth chattering in spite of the warm room, and Beltz went to the bar and poured them each a small glass of Napoleon brandy. She sipped slowly.

"Better?" he asked.

She nodded. "I love all this attention, but I need some answers."

"We have plenty of time for that," he said soothingly, "I want you to rest and get over the last few days."

"I'll be fine. I'm fine now. So humor me and tell me about Bob and Ellie. What really happened? Did you ever find out?"

Beltz threw his hands up. "You're a piece of work, you know that? You never let go. Okay, okay. Just yesterday Dr. Bergman, remember him? Ellie's doctor in the hospital? called me because Ellie's mind had cleared for almost a whole day. She talked to him quite openly about the accident at the governor's office, the words spilling out so fast he could hardly write them down. But he read me what she had told him."

Beltz took a long sip, finishing his brandy, and continued, "You won't believe it, but this is how it happened, according to Ellie. It seems she and Bob had been fighting ever since the truth about his affair came out, and really exploded the morning of the visit with the governor. She admitted saying things that infuriated him. It must have blown his usual cool, and he was in a murderous rage, her words, by the time they were leaving Rupert's office. She sensed this, and as they pushed their way through the crowd, trying to reach the elevator, she realized they were too close to the railing over the atrium. She turned around to tell him this and suddenly felt his hands pushing on her back. From the expression on his face, Ellie said, it was easy to figure out what was in his mind. She sidestepped quickly and Bob lost his balance, slamming into the railing, and the thrust of his forward motion propelled him over the side."

"Then Bob was really going to murder her? Serves him right, I think."

"I suppose you can look at it that way," Beltz conceded. "He'd been up to no good for some time."

"What'll happen to her?"

"I think it can be considered self-defense. More brandy?"

Molly offered her glass. "And George the Chief? What about him?"

"Well, he was a prime suspect in the beginning."

"When wasn't he?"

"When we learned about the other lover, and I found that bracelet signed Bob."

"And I found Bob," Molly boasted. "Am I given credit? Some kind of recognition that I was instrumental in solving your case."

Beltz laughed. "Why do you think I gave you the badge? But remember, this is your last case."

"Maybe."